Djibouti
Pier 17

A mystery set in the Horn of Africa

Leland L. Jones

A New Day Publishing
Atlanta

Soft Cover Edition

ISBN 978-0-9831695-0-5

First Edition 2010.

Printed in the United States of America.

Djibouti Pier 17 by Leland L. Jones

Published by: A New Day Publishing
www.anewdaybooks.com

<u>Acknowledgement</u>

To the People of Djibouti (who made me feel like royalty); to Service Personnel around the globe (of whom I have been); to Institutions of Higher Learning (which nurture raw talent); to Hassan Sugal (who provided understanding to Islam and Arabic); to Ms. Carmen who cared enough to set me on course, to A New Day Book Publishing (for taking a chance), and to adventure (may it ever be my friend).

DJIBOUTI PIER 17

(ji bōōt' ē)

<u>ONE</u>

Djibouti, Africa, Monday, February 26, 2007, 6:17 P.M.

"What's up Professeur? It's me, Maxi!"

Since Christmas Day of 2006 my Monday routine has generally consisted of a day of research at a location deemed the "hottest place on the planet year-round" followed by time in the laboratory and then to the Menelik where I'd open the window to my third floor hotel apartment which faces the Square and begin checking notes and downloading photos from the digital camera and placing them into the appropriate computer file folders. Around six o'clock I'd hear the distinctively raspy voice of a little boy who has been forced to grow up much too quickly and today is no different.

"Hey Lil' Buddy, wait there." I run downstairs only to find that someone from the hotel or one of the cab drivers had shooed him away from the immediate area.

Stepping into view I hear, "Hey Professeur, I'm over here."

Dressed in a macawiis, the traditional manskirt, of purple and red and sporting a plain yellow short sleeve shirt, the only thing traditional about Maxi is his attire. The contrast of his smooth and dark skin against his naturally blonde hair isn't the norm in Djibouti. Peculiar looking actually. His given name is Maximillion Abdi Ahmed and he's ten years old. He, like many other Djiboutian children, is fluent in Arabic, French, and "Somaleeze" but his use of English is quite impressive. He serves as the leader of a group of about fifteen to twenty young boys and girls who roam the streets. He refers to them as his "Posse." Though he is slight in stature he displays the swagger of someone twice his age and size. Jittering around like a big city gangster, our encounters usually begin the same.

"Hey, what's up Professeur?" We shake hands and hug, a manhug that is, complete with back slap.

"Not much happenin' Lil' Buddy. What's up with you?"

"Same old thing, you know. Tryin' to make a dollar. Stayin' out of trouble, you know what I'm sayin'?"

I once asked him how his English had become so "urbanized" and his response was classic Maxi, "Rap music, know what I'm sayin'?"

Enough said.

Despite our limited time together, our conversations always lead back to one central question, "How was school today?"

"Its alright. Matter of fact, I got my paper back from the Science test I took last week. I did good, ya know? I really appreciate the help you gave me."

It's difficult to hold a comfortable conversation or to tutor Maxi in his studies because the stores and restaurants won't allow locals to come inside nor do they want them to congregate outside of their establishments. I'd usually get ice cream, fruit or a couple of bags of chips from the convenient store and we'd eat and talk while sitting on the curb.

He says he lives somewhere in the area. A few weeks ago he introduced me to two little girls, Malika and Najat, and a little boy named Rockefeller, nicknamed Rocky. Each with smooth mahogany skin and crowned with whispy blonde hair. "Hey Professeur I want you to meet my little sisters and my little brother. I be lookin' out for em' ya know." He could have cancelled the familial declaration because of their obvious similarities. Little Rocky even had Maxi's movements and stance down pat.

The little ones said nothing but the obvious look of love and respect given to their big brother spoke volumes. According to Maxi there are five children in his family, the three younger and one older. He says his mother is very sick so he and his siblings do what they can to help provide money and food. Being the hustler,

I realize that he could be lying about his mom being sick but here is where trust is exercised.

Intelligent and spirited, the hustler in this kid sometimes appears from out of no where. In the middle of our conversation about World Literature a slight grin appears as he lowers his voice and leans towards me. "I got what you need." He reaches into his worn and tattered backpack and pulls out a box of Monte Christo cigars and a few videos with current titles. I know the movies are bootlegs and the cigars are knock-offs but so what. I hand him a twenty. "Good lookin' out Lil' Buddy."

We walk toward the large tree at the center of the square and five smiling children approach. Posse members.

"Have you kids done your school work?"

Maxi translates, *"Madrasa 'amal."*

They nod and do their best to mimic the movements of Maxi, "Yeah, yeah, man its cool. It's cool." Their response never really answers the question but I give them each a dollar anyway.

"Hey Maxi, special order. Bring me something nice for my mother's birthday."

"What kinda stuff she like?"

"Woman stuff."

Without hesitation he reaches into his backpack and pulls out the most beautiful red and gold embroidered shawl. He shows me the label. "100% Cashmere. Hand-made in India. This what you want?"

"Perfect!" Another twenty.

Shaking hands, he confirms, "Next week right?"

"You know where to find me." Manhug. "I'm proud of you Lil' Buddy. Stay out of trouble and make good choices."

"For sure. For sure." Head bobbing.

He begins to walk away with the Posse close behind.

I watch as each child disappears into the shadows.

Gone.

<u>TWO</u>

Thursday, March 1, 2007, 3:49 P.M.

A thermometer reading of 128° Fahrenheit doesn't seem so bad when the headphones are blasting *"Born under a Bad Sign"* by Jimi Hendrix in your ear. Sweat pours and at the end of the day my shirt displays the chalky stains where potassium has escaped. Bilal, my Djiboutian translator and guide, sweats not a drop. Here we are at Lac Assal, one of the hottest places on the planet and he never sweats. He consistently wears long trousers and short sleeve shirts but never have I seen him perspire. Slight in stature, his darkened skin is dry and relaxed, much like his demeanor. Having graduated from the Université de Djibouti, his practical and professional insights to my research have proven invaluable.

Lac Assal is French for "Lake of Salt" and that is exactly what it is, a large lake with crystal clear water and a gleaming and bumpy bed of white. Salt. My University, Clarkmore in Atlanta, has given me a year to conduct research and for the last three and half months I have ridden the bumpy and narrow road 75 miles west of Djibouti City to this hellishly hot place that rest 511 feet below sea level in the Afar Depression. This area was published as being, "One of the worst places on the planet to sustain life." I personally found such a statement to be broad, arrogant and small minded. The research seemed unfounded because the record of existence shows that the animal kingdom constantly displays the ability for living elements to adapt to their environments. My opinion became public in an Op-Ed piece, and the challenge was issued. My purpose here is to find a species of animal, or insect, that is not identified and not categorized but has adapted and thrived in this harsh environment. I am an educator and a scientist and here is where I will render a great contribution to the world of scientific investigation.

To date, I have found nothing. I remain hopeful that my efforts will not be in vain. The daily process is tedious but I go forward looking to find that which is not. That has become my mantra and I have it written on every notebook I've used, "WHEN I FIND WHAT ISN'T, IT WILL BE!"

Routinely, Bilal and I, travel to Lac Assal for the purpose of investigating the three research sites that I have established. On average we are here for about five to six hours each day.

Totally engrossed in my work, I am oblivious to the time. Bilal taps me on the shoulder and calls to me in English,

"Professor. Professor!" I can't hear him because I'm wearing my usual pair of old-school and oversized headphones and the music is blasting but I generally know what he is saying as he jestures toward his watch, "It is time!"

Turning the music on helps me to shut out the world around me. I get lost in the rhythms and it somehow activates a world within that helps me to dig a little deeper. The same routine is applied when I'm in the lab. Headphones on, I dig a little deeper. In the field of research it's all about focus but having been alerted as to the time, I wrap the cord to the headphones around the Nano and begin over-stuffing my backpack.

Bilal walks over and talks with Na'im, the head of the local clan. It amazes me that in this crop deprived and comfort barren terrain there resides a family that sells items to visitors at Lac Assal. At the sound of a vehicle they appear from over the ridge and stand beside the entrance to the lake where flimzy tables have been placed. Their wares are handmade souvenirs. Carvings made out of soft stone along with geodes found in the lake and cut in half to reveal the crystallized beauty within, there are natural salt crystals, which shimmer in the sunlight, and odd looking salt crystal sculptures that are created when objects, usually animal skulls, are submerged in the lake for long periods of time. This process forms a pure white crystallized coating of salt that covers the object. Some call it art. I call it spooky.

The sons of Na'im, Nadir and Yasir, appear from over the ridge to conduct business while their father is talking with Bilal. The boys, late teens or early twenties, have taken over the daily duties of swimming the lake and canvassing for objects to be crystallized and harvested on submerged cords. The boy's ability to hold their breath and dive to incredible depths, wearing only goggles, and searching the lake floor is amazing. They perform their duties with skill and determination doing what is needed to help provide for their family. It looks like difficult work and they do it well.

Bilal once shared with me that Na'im could best his sons in diving any day. He is thin and short, always clad in a manskirt and a shirt of any choosing. His body density is quite minimal but his hands and his feet are not just large, they are thick. Walking with no shoes can account for the feet, but his hands look as if they could break rocks with one quick blow. I never really try to talk to Na'im, that's Bilal's department. I do try to support his family enterprise, "Two dollars." Smiling through darkened teeth, he nods and the deal is done.

Larger items. "I will give you fifteen dollars."

He nods and smiles through darkened teeth, "Twenty." I am convinced that he knows no other English except for dollar amounts. His two sons have also learned the merits of a firm price yet their English is far more advanced that their father's.

We usually arrive at Lac Assal with a case of bottled water for Na'im and his family. A gesture of continued appreciation. I've established three research sites in the area, and it is hoped that these small gestures will help to keep things in order. So far, so good.

I walk past the two of them and sling my heavily laden backpack into the rear of our Mitsubishi SUV. Vials, small containers, brushes, magnifying glass, tweezers, tools, digital camera, cassette recorder, tapes, a butterfly net and always a spiral ringed notebook with blue *BIC* inkpens. I'm not superstitious but these inkpens have helped me to earn my best grades since high school.

I don't regret leaving around 3 o'clock in the afternoon, because its Thursday and I have to be at the Horsed School in the Balbala district to participate in the English Discussion Group.

Driving back to the City, I am reminded of how my introduction to Bilal, my Menelik apartment, my collaboration with the U of Djibouti and my participation in the English Discussion Group was due to U.S. Ambassador Daniel Singleton.

●●●●●●●●●●●●

When I was preparing to come to Djibouti I needed Security Clearance for the project which required approval from the American Embassy and Ambassador Singleton. I wrote him a letter outlining my purpose and seeking acceptance. Three pages, all business. Ambassador Singleton wrote back, "Access granted, but you must dine at my residence periodically." Done.

I arrive at the Aeroport International deDjibouti, loaded my two duffle bags into a taxi and was headed to Embassy. What little I saw of the city that day was underwhelming. Dirty. But my first view of the coast reversed my initial impression. Spectacular.

The Ambassador's residence possessed the visual elements of what an embassy should look like. Exuding importance. Austere. Immaculate. That said, I was relieved to see a group of about 40 people having a cookout in the backyard. Music blasting. Ribs simmering. Potato salad in abundance. Cold beer. Notions of jet-lag quickly faded.

The Ambassador greeted me in the yard. He had a million dollar smile and not a hair out of place. Black shoes shining, khaki trousers pleated, pressed and cuffed; light blue shirt button-down, no tie; blue blazer with golden buttons and a firm handshake. Think President Ronald Reagan holding a glass of iced cold lemonade. I had been in the city for little over an hour and I was sweating profusely but Ambassador Singleton never broke a sweat and he even kept his blazer on.

I thought, "Now this dude is cool." I soon came to find that to be the case, but I couldn't escape the notion that he seemed familiar. I reasoned that all white politicians tend to look the same to me. No offense.

"I hope I didn't disrupt the party?"

"Not at all, they probably don't notice you. Naval Reserve Unit from Louisiana. Going home next week. They've been stationed here at Camp LeMonier. You a military man?"

"Army. I did my time and got out. Desert Storm occurred a couple of months after I actually separated from the military and I kinda felt guilty, but not guilty enough to re-up."

"Officer?"

"Enlisted. I attended college afterward."

"Got your driver's license and passport?"

"Yes sir."

He hesitates, "Cool it with the 'Sir' crap. 'Ambassador' usually gets my attention."

"Yes sir...Ambassador...sir."

"What University are you with again?"

"Clarkmore in Atlanta, Georgia. It's one of the Historically Black Universities. I'm hoping my work here will attract dollars for the school's Science and Research Department."

"I hope you came to the right place. Tomorrow I'm taking you to Camp LeMonier to introduce you to some key people and get you a government ID. LeMonier is the only Combined Joint Task Force Operation in Africa. All military branches are represented. Its just a few minutes from here. Afterward we'll tour the town and I'll tell you where to go and where not to go.

"Thank you."

"Have you secured housing?"

"I had an arrangement but it fell through a few days ago and I…"

"Don't worry about it. You'll be staying at the Menelik Hotel. Center of town. Nice place. Lot's of history."

"Thank you, sir…Ambassador, but I don't want to…"

"Professor Dunstin let me make this point clear so that there will be no misunderstanding, Djibouti, Africa might not be a well-known location to the rest of the world, but for the next few years, it's where I call home. I will not have any embarrassing international incidents on my watch. I do my best to keep tabs on all of the Americans in this little country and if something isn't quite right I expect you to relay the same to me. Help me to help you to help these good people. Tonight, you'll stay here. I'll get someone to take your bags upstairs. For now, enjoy the party."

"Thank you, Ambassador."

Lifting his glass and flashing that million dollar smile, "It's the American people's house. You're always welcome."

An elegant woman peeks her blonde head out of the side door, "The steaks are getting cold, dear."

"Coming sweetie." He looks at me, smiles and winks. "Mrs. Ambassador." Enough said.

●●●●●●●●●●●●

I first met with Ambassador Singleton on November 28th of last year. His insights and connections have helped me to focus on my work. He connected me with Bilal. He helped to foster my relationship with the Sciences Department at the Université de Djibouti. With other Nationals in the city I participate in an English Discussion Group. "A way of giving back" he said.

EDG sessions are held throughout the week at various locations, but I have chosen to participate in the session that gathers every Thursday evening at the Horsed School. Parents, Djiboutian or Ethiopian, save money and send their children to these evening schools which are an addendum to their normal school day. The purpose at EDG is to learn to speak English in an English speaking environment. The kids range from age five to twenty-five with differing levels of English proficiency. When the students enter the yard, English only. Classroom walls made of plywood. Scraps basically. Four rooms side by side, each with six worn and rickety wooden benches that will hold five to seven students. On the chalkboard is the subject for the day's discussion.

"How do you feel about American clothing?"

"How do you feel about the display of affection on TV?"

"What would you like to be when you get older?"

"Are the roles of women changing in Djibouti daily life?"

The dialog is honest and insightful. Nonpolitical and nonreligious. Two or three American volunteers per room with twenty to thirty Djiboutian youth. Amazing. Each child speaks French, Arabic and "Somaleeze" while their English vocabulary is expanding impressively. The children thoughtfully express their points of view.

Esam says, "I want to be a race car driver."

Not surprising, Fatinah asserts, "I want to be a lawyer." She argues very well, especially with the boys in the room.

Zahrah doesn't hesitate, "I want to become a journalist." Her eloquence will find its outlet.

"In my humble opinion, I think I will be a football player." Soccer is played everywhere, but if anyone can make it onto the national team, it will be Thaqib. He comes to class every Thursday with a soccer ball and wearing flip-flops.

The reality for some of these children will be the same for many others around the world. Big dreams followed by harsh realities. Many of these kids won't make it to the local University, or any other institution of higher learning. For that matter, many of them won't make it out of Djibouti City or off the Continent. Many will have to start working to help with the household. Some dreams will be deferred, others dashed, but nothing can dismiss the fact that at this moment in time, they are working toward dream fulfillment and I am more impressed with each personal encounter.

When we arrive at the Horsed School, Bilal seems giddy. Happy for no apparent reason. Very loose and talkative. I have also noticed that during the hour that I spend with the youth he is nowhere to be found but when class is over he's leaning on the Mitsu. Grinning from ear to ear.

We leave the school and he drops me off at the Menelik. I am grateful to the Ambassador for setting me up in this prime location. It's in the heart of town, right on the Square. Great place for people watching. It's an older hotel, adequate for my needs. It's comfortable, and most important, air-conditioned. The standard sized bed, chair, and table set-up. Their restaurant is one of the best for basic cuisine, but I found out the hard way that the fancier the food the looser the bowels. Stick with the chicken and avoid the local fish. This is the commercial district. There are shops and restaurants of various types. Clothing. Souvenirs. Nite clubs. The open market is three blocks away, but I haven't taken the time to go and buy anything because I have Maxi. If I need something he gets it for me. I help him. He helps me.

Before Bilal leaves I remind him, "Tomorrow we go to the University."

"What time?"

I don't know why he asks about time, because he's always late. "Nine." I responded knowing that eleven is the time we are expected to be there. Telling him nine might get us there on time.

With great respect, I have found that the issue of time with Bilal, and other Muslims, is centered around their ritual prayer called *Salah* or *Salat*. It is performed five times a day.

I found that the time of prayer changes periodically according to the position of the sun and it is announced by the muezzin from the mosque's minaret. Though the actual times will vary, prayer is to be performed at dawn, midday, afternoon, sunset and evening. I learned to never ask Bilal to work on Fridays because that is the Muslim "Holy Day" when he is expected to join in congregational prayer with fellow Islamic believers in Allah.

It has been said that "Routine is the friend of the Researcher" and though my efforts have not produced the desired results I am confident that my routine of consistent study and documentation will prove my hypothesis and my procedures to be effective. I am closer to reaching my goal.

Sadly, the same routine that will bring me success has also left me wanting. I have been in Djibouti for almost four months and though I have found ways to break the monotony, I am beginning to experience a lack of fulfillment.

Lonely.

THREE

Wednesday, March 21, 2007, 10:45 A.M.

Bilal arrives. *"As-salaamu alaikum."*

"Wa 'alaikum as-salaam."

Driving to the campus we are careful to avoid the people that are gathering around the khat stands. Each person willingly surrendering their hard earned wages for the reddish root with the avocado green colored leaves. Concerning khat, freshness matters. The fresher the khat the more potent the response. The purchase and exchange of khat is frenzied and sometimes combative. It is customary that only the men chew khat. The woman can purchase it for a man, but she is not allowed to partake, at least in public. With each purchase I'd see men fitting the green leafy bundles into their pockets only to release them at the end of the day and begin the process of rolling the bitter root into a ball and fitting it into the jaw. The chewing and grinding on the unassuming and ill tasting foliage develops into an unsightly green residue that begins to form around the corners of the mouth. Unpleasant. The constant chewing of khat causes the teeth to blacken. Not a little dingy. Black! The other effects of khat are displayed by men throughout the country as they become overly energized and animated, then agitated, then devoid of energy. Wasted. This is followed by a major case of the munchies, sugar being the target. Late in the day, the lethargy of the khat chewer is hard to dismiss. For these reasons it is outlawed in ninety percent of the African countries, khat is generally classified as a drug and it brings on a "high" that is cheap, low grade and appreciated daily. The long term effects are much more damaging and though there is debate over the findings, it has been noted that the majority of the men that chew khat will have issues with diabetes, impotence, and dental destruction. The physical response is one thing but the collective effects in an impoverished country cannot be dismissed. Daily use of khat makes for a collective nonproductive period that is condoned by society, but good for no one.

Bilal mutters, "Khat come early today."

The khat to Djibouti arrives daily from Ethiopia in a green and white cargo plane. Distinctive and unmistakable. The fresh shipment usually arrives in the morning. The bundles are packed into large white bags and workers unload enough to usually fill three very large truckloads. From the airport it goes to the local distribution factory where it is immediately packaged and sent to the streets for daily consumption.

"Bilal, why don't you chew khat like everybody else?"

Shaking his head, "I see what it does. Takes you up. Lets you down. Takes your money."

Jokingly I respond, "Well, if your teeth begin to turn black, I will know more than I will want to know." I laugh as he grins broadly, showing all of his teeth. White, sorta.

I consider Bilal a friend. I haven't made many acquaintances since coming to Djibouti, but my focus is not to be sociable. I am here to conduct research and I have established a consistent regiment of work, work, and more work. At this time in my life the casual friendship or even intimate relationships are considered hindrances. I've learned to establish associations that are cordial, low maintenance and easy to manage, anything more would be considered an impediment to success. That being said, we arrive at the Université de Djibouti for lab research and to visit a colleague that I have grown to appreciate.

I generally spend three to five hours in the lab so I exit the vehicle with backpack in hand, "Bilal, I'll call you when it's time."

"Nabad." He drives away.

I walk up to the third floor. The Biology Department. Professeur Henrì Dublé is expecting me.

I enter the room, big smiles. "Bonjour, Professeur Dunstin. Come in. Come in. You made it here right on time." With cane in hand he manages to stand. Suspenders holding up his baggy brown khaki trousers, complete with red checkered shirt and crooked blue bow tie. His white tennis shoes squeak and scuff the floor as he begins to shuffle toward the cabinet in the back of the room. He waves me on, "Come with me Professeur."

"It's too early for that Professor Dublé."

"*S'il vous plait*. It is never too early for a glass of fine Sherry." His eyes of gray begin to sparkle.

"Too rich for my taste. When you have a cedar lined Merlot, call me."

"*Oui, en effet*. Found something new have you?"

"Only a few specimen worthy of investigation."

"As always *mon ami*, the lab is yours. Do you have your key?"

I check my pockets, "*Oui Professeur.*"

Looking over his glasses, which are resting on the bridge of his nose, "I have class, followed by meetings." Sweat beginning to bead on his pale and balding white forehead, he moves towards the door, cane in the right and briefcase in the left. "You know where to find me when you make your big discovery and it is time to celebrate."

"*Merci, Professeur Dublé.*"

He exits.

I go to the door of my office space and with the turn of the key, I enter the Zone. Headphones on. Nano on full blast. *"The Devil went down to Georgia"* plays as I find myself hollering, "Sing it Charlie Daniels…hell yeah!" My feet, my hands and even my mind move to the rhythm of the song. *"He was in a bind, he was way behind, he was willing to make a deal."* I've uploaded country, rock, jazz, gospel, R & B, soul, funk, and even some Classical. My musical taste are not eclectic, I just like what I like.

I open the backpack and retrieve the Canon A530, corked vials, small containers of dead insects, plant life, minerals and salt fragments to be examined. Two to three times a week for the last three and a half months I spend investigative time in the Zone. I've been given a small space to work and I've also been given the free reign of the laboratory, the library, and the computer lab. My relationship with the Biology Department of the Université de Djibouti creates a working relationship Clarkmore University and it is due to the efforts of the Ambassador, but no one could have arranged for the mutual respect that Professor Dublé and I share.

The research space that I've been given is complete with a window facing the classroom. It contains the minimum needed to perform my duties, a small desk, a chair, two short lab tables. One of the tables has a 3'x 4'x 3' glass examination enclosure complete with rubber arms and outside exhaust capabilities. It looks like a big aquarium. Luckily the room is sound proof, so my singing and my recitation bother no one. Most important, the room has a lock.

Though Professor Dublé and I don't engage in time wasting chit-chat about mundane affairs, I am most grateful for the scientific relief and challenge that only a colleague can bring. When visiting his office I am made to remember my days at Buchtel High School where, under the direction of Ms. Shriver, I came to enjoy everything about Science. His desk and shelves exhibit the evidence of a working teacher's world. Stacks of papers, some graded some not. Jars housing dissection victims. Frogs, oversized worms, and the ever-popular fetal calf (the fetal pig is a no go in Muslims countries). Reference books aplenty, mingled with tropical plants under lamps, beakers, a microscope, sealed bottles filled with labeled chemical solutions, $CH_2(COOH)_2$, $CHCl_3$, CH_3OH, and of course, the empty bottle which is theoretically filled with O_2. Add to all of this, the 3' x 4' version of the Periodic Table of the Elements on one wall and the 4' x 5' map of the world on the opposite wall complete with stringed travel markers, and you have the office of an educator. Dublè is helpful in that he has an easy way of turning "shop talk" into questions that keep me on the road to discovery.

"How are you preserving your specimen?"

"Are your notes timely?"

"Have you updated your research methods?"

It's 4:30 P.M., almost six hours after entering the Zone. Dublè returns. My door is open so he pops his head in and asks, "Anything new?"

"No. The search continues." Disappointment obvious.

He reassures, "Take heart *mon ami* you'll find it…whatever the hell *IT* is." He smiles then exits leaving the door open.

I step out of the Zone to phone Bilal. Reception is poor so I wander until connected. Returning to gathering my things, I hear Dublé arguing in French with a female. I secure the room and lock the door. Backpack in hand I round the corner to find him talking with an exquisitely beautiful brown skinned beauty.

I interrupt to say goodbye, *"Pardon. Au revoir, Professeur."*

Grudgingly he makes introduction, "Excuse my lack of manners. Professeur Carter Dunstin. Mademoiselle Lizette Moniette. He is an American researcher and scientist. She is a French real estate agent and a very stubborn negotiator. She was just leaving."

I extend my hand, "Pleased to meet you Mademoiselle."

"She was *JUST* leaving." Dublé confirms.

She glares, "Damn you Dublé." She turns and walks out. Her scent of roses and sandalwood lure my senses.

He stops me, "Dunstin. Her beauty is surface. Underneath is a very troubled woman. Avoid her. I warn you as a friend."

"Thank you for the insight Dublé, but I refuse to be distracted from my work."

He smiles and extends his hand. "Merlot, next time?"

"I look forward to it."

I begin walking down the hallway as my nose and imagination are filled with her scent. I don't see her as I enter the stairwell, but I hear the door shutting below. She exits and through the glass door I see the shape of an exotic beauty, dressed with care. Business yet sexy. She walks toward the curb, her thin and shapely frame moving with the rhythm of the Continent.

Bilal stands by the car.

Having exited the building, I walk toward her, "It was a pleasure to meet you."

She snorts, "Yes. It was."

Being cordial, "I have room if you need a ride."

She looks me up and down, "You a friend of Dublé?"

"Colleague. Professional acquaintance. Why do you ask?"

"Did he send you?"

Her attitude was more than I could tolerate, "Here's money for a taxi." I hand her a ten dollar bill. "Let's go Bilal." Getting into the Mitsu I look over my shoulder and notice Dublé watching us from his office window. The gesture of driving away without her was more for him to see than for her to experience. His advice was heeded and I really don't have time for distractions. Deuces.

<u>FOUR</u>

Wednesday, March 21, 2007, 7:41 P.M.

Riding with Bilal and rounding the corner to the Menelik, I see Maxi and Rocky sitting on the curb. This is the first time I have ever seen Maxi so stationary and something about this picture didn't seem right. "Bilal stop!"

"Professeur, did we forget something?"

"No." I reach over the seat and open the back door, "Maxi! Rocky! Get in!"

They look up and having recognized me they each manage a faint smile. Shoulders slumped and lacking the normal vigor, they climb into the vehicle.

"Hey, Professor what's up man?"

Bilal listens, but says nothing.

"I'm good Lil' Buddy, what's up with you and Maxi, Jr?"

"We just got back from seeing our moms at the hospital. She's not doing so good and they are thinking about sending us kids to someone in the family across the Gulf in Obock. My mother says it will help her to get better because then she won't have to be worried about us. You know what I'm sayin' right?"

"Yeah. I understand. When do you guys plan to move?"

"I don't know but before we go I gotta do something real nice for you, cause you been real good to me and my Posse. Helping us with schoolwork and all." He pauses and reflects, "I don't mind having to leave because I know I can come back, I just wonder whose gonna take care of my Posse. Ya know?"

"I'm sure you will prepare them to look out for one another and of course I'll be around to talk to them about their grades and anything else they might want to talk about. Another good thing is that me and my friend Bilal can drive around the Gulf to Obock to check on you guys. Isn't that right Bilal?" I hadn't really noticed, but Bilal was tightly clutching the steering wheel with an agitated expression on his face. He said nothing.

Maxi continues, "Professor, I appreciate it and I'll let you know what's up."

I hand him a few of dollars. "Peace."

Exiting the vehicle, Rocky turns, "Peace."

Having stopped in front of the Menelik, I look over at Bilal, as if to read his mind, "What?!"

"Professeur it is not wise to get involved with these low-lifes. They are thieves and liars. I'll bet there is nothing wrong with their mother, and another thing…"

"Stop! Just stop! Tomorrow we go to Lac Assal. Be here early." I grab my backpack and exit the vehicle. Turning back, "I appreciate your concern Bilal, but my connection with these 'low-lifes' is helping me to maintain my sanity. They are good kids. Don't ever disrespect them. Get some rest. Tomorrow. Early."

He says nothing.

"We good!?"

"Be careful Professeur."

I smile. Extend a hand, "*As-salaamu alaikum.*"

"*Wa 'alaikum as-salaam.*"

<u>FIVE</u>

Thursday, March 22, 2007, 8:45 P.M.

This has been a long day. Research at Lac Assal, followed by EDG and the weight of knowing that my Lil' Buddy would soon be leaving. I need to unwind.

Leaving the Balbala District, I asked Bilal to drop me off at my "Special Place." Knowing the most direct route he drives through the downtown district where the old European architecture is now decaying and is seriously in need of repair.

We pass the water de-salinization plant which works to transform the water of the Gulf into water for drinking. Good luck.

We pass the herds of livestock that are being taken to the Port de Djibouti for sale then to be loaded onto ships for transport. The Port is busy all day as it serves as the center of the country's import and export business.

We then pass the public beach area where it is not uncommon to find locals bathing.

Having passed all of the sights and sounds of daily Djiboutian life, we arrive at the nicest oasis in this desert. The Kempinski Palace Resort.

The only five-star resort in the country, the Kempinski truly lives up to its reputation. To be sure, you will pay top dollar for the services provided but it will be worth every penny and you will not go wanting. The Kempinski is my place to relax and to get away from Djibouti while in Djibouti. My Special Place.

I can't site one characteristic that is any more exceptional than the others. Upon arrival one is greeted by a 6'5" Ethiopian man who eloquently speaks several languages with which to make all guests feel at ease. His physical prowess accented by his stately demeanor and his princely garb gives one a feeling of royalty.

The multi-cultural front desk and support staff also lend itself to cultivating of an atmosphere of being far away from everyday Djibouti. The insightful ability of the well maintained Concierge to hear, to know and to make things happen in different cities, countries and Continents is a skill most appreciated.

The African and Arabian décor. The gold and marble water fountain at the entrance highlighted by a lightshow. The hand-made chandeliers twinkling with elegance.

The various restaurants that are fully capable of making exactly what you desire according to taste. Mediterranean. Asian. European. Regional. What one likes, they can prepare.

Their wine list must be the best in the Country. Bar none.

I really can't point to any one thing. The ambiance. The rooms. The beds. Oh my.

It all works together but the clincher for me is the view from the terrace overlooking the pool to the Gulf of Aden and the Gulf of Tadjoura. Magnificent.

Bilal drops me off at the front entrance. "How long?"

"It is late, you go home. Tonight I'll catch a taxi. Pick me up at eight in the morning. We go to Lac Assal. *Nabad.*"

Sadly, Bilal is not allowed in the lobby of the hotel, nor anywhere on the premises except for the parking lot. He's a local. No other reason. There are strict laws prohibiting commingling in certain public places and for him the penalty would be a fine, or imprisonment.

The Kempinski, Merlot and a good cigar. My download.

●●●●●●●●●●●●

The brief encounter with Lizette lingered in the back of my mind and it caused me to think about the last time I enjoyed the company of a woman. It was about three months ago. Late in the evening while walking through town I passed one of the dance clubs. Beautiful women stood outside and I went in. I ordered a few drinks and danced a little and before leaving our eyes met.

She sat in the corner with two other young women. Each from Ethiopia and each was absolutely gorgeous. She approached. "My name is Sahar." She stood close. Nice smell. I gently touched her arm. Soft. Tender. She spoke English.

"Call me Dixon." Every man has to have an alias.

We leave the club and though the Menelik was near I rented a room from another hotel for the night. We cuddled, caressed, talked and laughed. She wanted to hear stories about America and I just wanted the companionship. Into the early hours of the morning we enjoyed one another's company. We didn't engage in sex but I enjoyed the connection we were making.

There was a momentary lull in the conversation. It was around 4 o'clock in the morning, her head was on my exposed chest and she spoke ever so softly, "I would really love to go to America one day."

Uh oh.

I did my best to change the direction of the conversation, "America's a nice place, but I like Africa better.."

She ignored my derailment, "Could you help to get me there?"

In that instant, I realized that I had allowed the desire for temporary companionship to ruin my judgment. Damn! I said nothing.

Eager this time, "Could you take me when you go back?"

"Uhhhhh, I plan to be here for a while, so we will see." My hesitance elicited an uneasy silence.

Then, from out of nowhere, that tender moment was quickly replaced by attitude and anger unexpected. Loud and angry.

"So what do you want to do tonight cause I still get paid regardless!"

I said nothing.

She mockingly slowed her cadence, even made sign language gestures, as if I was not comprehending her words, "What…do…you…want…me…to…do…for…you?"

I laid there. Silent. After a few uncomfortable moments of her Jekyll and Hyde routine, I got up. I buttoned my shirt, fastened my belt, and put on my shoes. I gave her a hundred dollar bill and I lustfully watched as she covered her magnificent mocha brown skin with a black cat-suit along with black high heels and a waist jacket. Perfect hour-glass. So sexy. So disappointing. She left.

Moments later, I left.

I knew where I was. I knew what she was. I had hoped for something different. Temporary but different. Looking back on it, I just needed a friend but there was no excuse for my poor judgment. I know the statistics, the dominant number of the young woman in those clubs are sex slaves trying to earn enough to buy their freedom. Add to that sad fact, the number of HIV+ cases in

Africa are growing exponentially because of what I *almost* did, and had the "Bronx" not jumped out of that African beauty I too might be a statistic. Lesson learned.

•••••••••••

Tonight I sit on the deck and close my eyes. The Gulf of Aden is before me. Moon is hanging high. Merlot in my left. Stogie in my right. Shoes off with feet elevated. Relaxed.

I then hear the sweetest sound.

"Professeur Dunstin?"

Flowing with the breeze, I detect the scent of rose mingled with sandalwood. *"Bonsoir Mademoiselle Moniette."*

I stand, extending my hand. I kiss the back of hers. The olfactory is now overtaken by the ocular. She is absolutely stunning. Vivid brown eyes. Silky black middle of the back hair. Thin and succulent red lips. 5'9" or 5'10". Refined. Thin yet highlighted with curves in the right places. Perfect model-type posture. A yellow bikini top and bottom accentuate her statuesque appeal. The opening to her cream colored sarong with fringed edges parts ever so slightly to reveal legs that stir my imagination. Nice toes. Pink polish. Exquisite.

She asks, "Do you come here often?"

"Only to unwind. You?"

42

"I live near."

Without hesitation, "Care to join me?"

I motion for an attendant to bring her a chaise. She orders, "Champagne please. Dry."

She catches me off guard, "I love the smell of your cigar."

"I love the smell of you."

"A charmer."

Changing the tone of the conversation, "The other day I…"

"Say no more. That was then, let's enjoy now." She's smooth.

It did not take long for me to realize that the introduction from Dublé was hardly adequate. He said she was French, the truth is she is Creole born and raised in Praia which is the capital city of Cape Verde Island in West Africa. Portuguese is her native tongue but her proficient use of French and English help her to better navigate business dealings. She attended college in England. She is single. No children. And apparently she is one of the best realtors in the business. The company she works for is based in France, but she is considering severing ties and starting her own agency. Her competence is well established and if there is a major real estate deal in Djibouti or Ethiopia she is somewhere in the mix. Let her tell it, the rift with Dublé involves property prices and though he'd like more from their relationship, she finds him repulsive. "He's got sweaty palms."

After an hour of talking and enjoying one another's company I had to ask, "Would you mind having dinner with me one evening?"

"I would love to Professeur Dunstin."

"Please, call me Carter."

"I would love too…Carter."

"It's getting late. Care to share a taxi?"

"No. I live in walking distance."

"Mind if I walk you home?"

"I'd like that very much."

We leave Kempinski and continue talking and enjoying one another's company. Too soon, we reach her flat. I take the liberty of giving her a kiss her on the cheek. She accepts. "Good night."

I walk back to the Resort and catch a taxi to the Menelik.

Alone.

Content.

Hopeful.

Big grin, Cheshire Cat.

<u>SIX</u>

Monday, March 26, 2007, 6:25 P.M.

"What's up Professeur? It's me, Maxi with the Posse."

I emerge from the Menelik carrying a big box. I set it down on the ground and say nothing of it..

Having seen us together, it no longer angers the shopkeepers and business owners as it did before. They are fully aware of our purpose, and some have helped to facilitate our weekly gatherings. I send Maxi and Rocky to the convenience store to buy each kid a bag of chips. They return and we spend an enjoyable evening teaching one another. The way I see it, EDG is great for those who can afford it, so why not do the same with those who can't.

We gather at the big tree in the Square under the street light. These children are skilled at what they do to survive but under the big tree they bring their schoolwork, their hopes and dreams, and their questions concerning life. Under the big tree innocence is restored, even if temporary. These kids have developed skill-sets not exhibited by those who are considered well-off. These kids find strength to survive in conditions that would ontherwise bring discouragement. Despite their lack they press on and it is here under the big tree that they are welcomed, celebrated and embraced. Here, they are respected.

For the past four and a half months we have had insightful discussions regarding their class work and their lives. I don't tutor as much as I help to facilitate their ability to teach one another. The proverb is true when it instructs that, *"Most learn best, when they teach."*

Before they leave, "Maxi I want to thank you for letting your Posse be a part of our time together."

Classic Maxi, thumbs up and head bobbing, "It's cool Professeur. It's cool. Family ya know."

"Yeah…family. Before you go, I got something for each of you. I told some friends of mine in America about the good work you're doing in school, and they sent some things to encourage you." I open the box and pull out a brand new black and burgundy backpack, with the words Clarkmore University embroidered on the front. Each is filled with notepads, pencils, pens and a calculator. One for each child.

The kids are ecstatic! Even the on-looking taxi drivers and shop owners applaud the gesture.

Maxi says, "Line up." Obediently, from shortest to tallest they form a single file line. Each child steps forward and receives a backpack at which time they open their arms giving me a hug followed by a heart felt "Thank you."

Even Maxi, the king of cool, opens both arms and warmly gives and receives a hug. "Thank you Professeur. I'll never forget this."

Smiles on all. Then, as always, one by one they disappear. Fading into the shadows.

Gone.

<u>SEVEN</u>

Wednesday, March 28, 2007 6:55 P.M.

Another long day of research at Lac Assal. It's been hotter than normal, but I left normal back in Atlanta.

Bilal and I arrive at the Menelik. I see the children who are members of the Posse standing around and when I get out of the Mitsu and they running towards me. Each of them crying.

"Professeur! Professeur!" The tears. The sobbing. No one can articulate what is going on. We embrace. Correction, they cling. I embrace.

Something's obviously not right and an emptiness begins to overtake me. Tears beginning to well in my eyes.   Tragedy but in what form.

"Had Maxi been taken to Obock?"

"Is his mother alright?"

I need answers.

"Can someone please tell me what has happened."

Utbah tries to explain through his tears, "Maxi didn't want to work for them! But they said that he had to. He said no, but then they beat him. Nobody would help us!"

Not understanding what he was saying, I asked him to stop talking. "Shhhh. Talk slow Utbah. What happened?"

Little Azzah, wipes her tears and speaks, "They kill Maxi."

"What!?"

"They kill Maxi."

Bilal, who was talking with some of the taxi drivers hears the same and approaches, "Professeur, your friend Maxi. He is dead."

"No."

"Today, he was beaten to death. In the alley."

"By who? Why?"

"Professeur, the people are afraid and they are saying very little. They did tell me about what good things you have done for the children. I did not know. Right now, they are afraid and all they will say is, '*Al-qaanoon*' and '*Rashaaqa*'."

"What does that mean?"

"The men who did this are thugs. Very bad men. The people fear them. They call these men '*Al-qaanoon*' which means 'Law' and '*Rashaaqa*' which means 'Grace.'"

"Bilal, a little boy was beaten to death and no one but the kids tried to stop it!"

"The people are afraid. It is said that these men live by their own gruel laws, and they give grace only when they choose. The message in killing your friend was simply to intimidate the others."

Bilal continues talking to me. I look around and I notice that everyone, the children and the adults, begin to disappear. No one wants to be associated with these tragic happenings and so they leave.

Across the street, the last face I see is that of a tear stained Rocky.

Gone.

●●●●●●●●●●●●

Bilal gathers more information and attempts to help me to make sense of a senseless situation. He shares with me that Maxi was approached by two men. Both African. To the frightened people in the community the men are known as *Law* and *Grace*. They approached Maxi, and tried to force him to work for them and to be their "runner." Quitting school was a part of the deal and Maxi refused. He wouldn't take their money nor would he accept their offer. He attempted to run away and they grabbed his new backpack. He fought to get it back. The other children tried to help, and a few of them were hurt as well, but the children were little resistance. The men grabbed Maxi and they beat him with their bare fist. They stomped on him with their feet. They left him bloodied and unconscious. Clutching his new backpack, he died.

The tragedy was compounded by the fact that the thugs reportedly enjoyed beating the ten year old kid to death. They actually took pleasure in their public display of fear and intimidation. Witnesses note that the two laughed with every blow that landed and when Maxi's frail and limp frame fell to the ground the two continued kicking and stomping him, bouncing his skull off the ground and leaving him in a bloodied pool.

Someone even reported that they licked his blood from their knuckles and dared that a report be made to the Police.

They reportedly returned to their vehicle but one of them came back and made a point of retrieving the backpack and emptying its contents over the unrecognizable and lifeless crimson form.

Such barbarity. No one tried to help.

••••••••••••

Tears flowing. I go to my room and leave the window open. Hoping.

Silence.

Gone.

EIGHT

Wednesday, May 30, 2007, 7:09 P.M.

Maxi died two months ago.

The events of that day changed my view of the local community. I became disinterested, short tempered and frustrated with the normal flow of everyday life. Historically, the Square around the Menelik has been the cultural and social center of Djiboutian life since the early 1900s when the French claimed the territory and deemed it French Somaliland. Today, culture exist. Social interaction exist. Caring is lacking. People moving about in such a way that creates stagnation. No progress.

Maxi, my Lil' Buddy, was beaten to death in the alley and no one tried to help. Djibouti only, no way! The same is true in other cities, large and small, around the globe. Industrialized areas, rural domains, city landscapes and country vistas where people are hustling and some are being hustled. Some are hurt. Some thrive. Life.

Maxi is dead.

The investigation into his beating revealed that no one wanted to speak to the police, and the police really wanted not to be involved. A ten year old boy, known by all, is beaten to death and no one says a word to help to find his killers. My hurt and my outrage cannot be shaken way. I am disgusted.

The Posse members see me and they wave, but from a distance. They are afraid and are instructed to keep silent by their elders. I sit on the bench in the Square every Monday around six o'clock, only to have no one show up with their books, their homework, or their questions.

Sadder still, three days after Maxi was killed, his mother died of complications from AIDS. She had been in quarantine, and word of her son's death and her inability to attend the funeral only hastened the inevitable. Though her death certificate said that she died of pneumonia it would also have been correct if it noted that she died of a broken heart.

His siblings have been taken to family members across the Gulf in Obock and I have not seen them since.

Maxi was special to me because he was the kid I used to be. Gifted and enterprising, both of us needing someone to challenge and to direct our energies. I tried to give to him the magic that the special people in my life gave to me. The magic of knowing that I am special and that I am unique and gifted.

When Maxi died, something also died in me. I continued my work with purpose, but extracurricular activities seem less important. I have missed several of the Thursday night EDG meetings. I frequent the Kempinski less. I spent more time alone, or face down in my research.

The work at Lac Assal motivates me but the cowardice of the community disengages me and I find myself withdrawing from the one bright spot in my life, Lizette. We spend time with one another, quality time. I know she is trying to get me to open up but certain areas remained sealed. To her credit, she is patient and caring. She listens to what I say and tries to decipher what I don't say. We laugh and enjoy our time together. She's special but I have never shared with her the events surrounding my Lil' Buddy. Too painful.

My feelings for Lizette are real. If situations were different this would be the perfect relationship. I want to be loved. She wants me to love her. I want to be able to give love but I don't want a love so strong that it interferes with my work and my purpose for being in Djibouti. I also don't want a love that is abandoned after the research is ended.

I am reminded of the adage that, "A fool works hardest when placing limitations on love." Concerning Lizette, I am that fool.

I came here to conduct scientific research but now I fear that someone, like Maxi, will leave without warning. I don't think I could bear it.

<u>NINE</u>

Thursday, May 31, 2007, 11:27 A.M.

Entering Lac Assal, Bilal and I notice a large black Mercedes with tinted windows. It seemed out of place. In the urban districts around Djibouti City there are many different cars and buses that fill the streets, all makes and models, but the vehicles that travel to Lac Assal are generally fitted for the trip. Knobby tires. High ground clearance with the ability to handle the rocks and the bumpy roads of the outer regions. The black Mercedes was definately out of place. We were initially under the impression that the vehicle belonged to dignitaries then we noticed a yellow smiley face sticker on the rear window on the passenger side. The dignitary consideration was abandoned.

Na'im was talking with one of two men standing near the car. They both wore short sleeve shirts, dark shades, slacks, sandals, and they looked exactly alike. Literally. They were twins.

The one standing near the car lowered his glasses and eyed us carefully.

We slowly pulled up and parked not far from them, careful not to create a stir. I asked Bilal if he knew what was going on and he shrugged his shoulders.

He addressed the three men, *"As-salaamu alaikum."*

They responded, *"Wa 'alaikum as-salaam."*

We maintained our normal routine by unloaded the case of water for Na'im and set it on the table.

Na'im nodded. *"Shukran."*

"Afwan."

I retrieved my backpack, and we start toward Site III.

Walking away I hear Na'im say, *"Sadiq wa usstaz."* Loosely translated, "Friend and Professeur."

We reach the Site. Headphones on. The smooth jazz stylings of Grover Washington's *"Mister Magic"* then Dave Koz kicks in with *"You Make Me Smile."* The men with Na'im made me a bit uncomfortable but the music mellows my soul and works to center my mind on the task at hand. Let do this!

Bilal carried his prayer mat and a bottle of water. He said very little as he kept an eye on Na'im and the two visitors. He also appeared uncomfortable and it was obvious.

I looked back and observed Na'im pass two white cloth bags to one of the twins. The bags were the sizes of pillowcases. I was not alarmed, because I had seen him use these bags for other customers. Larger items were sometimes heavy and the cloth bags served the purpose of securing the purchased goods.

●●●●●●●●●●●●

Concerning each of the Sites, two days ago I placed a partially plucked raw chicken in a wire cage. The purpose was to see what it attracts. I intend to secure the samples from Sites I and II over the next two weeks to see if different insects might have visited throughout the various stages of decay.

Today's focus is Site III and the follow-up investigation revealed three flying insects that looked worthy of investigation. I use the A530 to take photographs and videos, while simultaneously using the audio cassette recorder to document my findings.

After five hours of research I use the folding spade to dig around the caged specimen and place the entire sample into a large ventilated plastic bag. Everything is included; the wire cage, the chicken, and anything that had attached itself to the chicken along with one to three inches of surface from under the specimen. I had hopes that insects would be trapped inside the bag and inside the carcass. After documenting each step in the notebook I use the magnifying glass to locate any odd fluids or other oddities. We gently begin to load the gear and our specimen.

59

Walking over the hill to the Mitsu I notice that the black Mercedes was gone.

A tour bus had arrived and I could hear their British accent. People were buying trinkets and mementos from Nadir and Yasir. Business was good. Some of the visitors came prepared with swimwear and were floating in the water. Others were tasting the water. Salty. Extremely salty.

Their guide exclaims, "On the way back, I'll show you the site where the 1970's movie, *The Planet of the Apes*, was filmed. The one with Charlton Heston."

Visitors to this area are given surface information about this amazingly desolate place but they don't get the insights that make it so special. So alive and unique. Lac Assal is a crater lake that is surrounded by dormant volcanoes. Black lava rocks that have been pushed to the surface by shifting tectonic plates are strewn all across the region in a variety of sizes. Lac Assal is also known for being hyper-saline, in fact it is the most saline body of water known to man, outside of Antarctica. Even more unique is the fact that Lac Assal doesn't have any streams feeding into it because its source is the hot bubbling springs from below that emanate from the Gulf of Tadjoura.

Some of the springs are too hot for the human touch but in the same pools I have seen fish swimming and thriving. Amazing.

"Planet of the Apes." I think to myself, "Rookies."

After loading the Mitsu, Bilal goes to Na'im and they engage in what would appear to be an argument. Hard to tell because in their culture the animated hands and the elevated voice and even the aggressive touching means very little. They speak in rapid fire Somaleeze and I understand not a word. Different here was when Bilal put his finger in the face of Na'im and was clearly rebuking him. Tourist are staring but Nadir and Yasir seem unconcerned and continue serving customers. I continue loading the vehicle.

A flustered Bilal returns to the vehicle. We enter and he starts the Mitsu. "Is everything alright?"

"What do you mean, Professeur?"

"What do you mean, what do I mean? You know what I mean, with you and Na'im."

"He asked if I can take three bags of salt to the market for selling. Tourist buy it after it has been placed into jars. I told him no."

"Why?"

"Once you say yes, you can never stop saying yes. It will be salt today, then something else the next time. I had to say no."

"Bilal, they live in a very remote area. No running water. No electricity. I don't really know how they can function in this constant and stifling heat. I am grateful for their cooperation and if there is some way that we can help I have no problem with it."

"No! We bring water every time we arrive, that is enough. Today salt to the market. Tomorrow who knows. No!"

•••••••••••

Thirty minutes into the drive to the Horsed School, "Professeur, I want to give you advanced notice that I will not be available this Saturday."

"No problem. Got plans?"

"Yes. I am to be wed."

"You're getting married?!"

"Does this surprise you?"

"No. I just haven't seen you around any women. Actually, we never talk about women. I thought you were disinterested."

"Business is business Professeur but I actually have you to thank for getting us together."

"What do you mean?" Feeling like a giddy little school girl I ask, "And what is her name?"

"Her name is Numa. She lives in the Balbala District, not far from the Horsed School."

Thinking openly, "So every Thursday for the past six months you've been spending time with Numa?"

He smiles shyly, and nods.

"Numa, that's a very pretty name. What does it mean?"

"It means beautiful and pleasant. She represents it very well. I have asked her father for consent and it has been given."

●●●●●●●●●●●

Before going to the Horsed School, we take the specimen to the Université. We both carry it up to the Zone and place it in the glass examination dome. Bilal then goes out of the room as I place a mask over my face and put on a paper lab coat. I shut the door and turn on the tape recorder and the A530. Video mode. The dome is secured and using the rubber gloved arms I carefully remove the bag from the specimen. I turn on the air compressor which pumps outside air into the dome. I set the artificial light sensors for 7 A.M. to 7 P.M. The temperature inside the enclosure is set at 80° Fahrenheit during the dark and 120° Fahrenheit during daylight. The light and temperature variations will gradually change over a half an hour. I thought I had secured the glass enclosure but when using the rubber gloved arms to open the bag to remove the specimen a bit of stink began seeping through. Today the odor is bad but in a few days it will be violent.

The carcass is already showing promise. Looking closely, I notice a few larva. A few flies. A few mites. Parasites, I'm sure. I don't know exactly what is there, but the answers will unfold in the next few days. Using the A530, I chronicle the tiny creatures draining their host. "Dinner is served." The foundation sample of salt, sand and rock is also placed in the container.

To better utilize the synthetic lighting schedule I place a black cloth over the container and I close the blinds to the window for privacy.

Dublè was not in the building so I tape a note to his office door. "Pr. Dublè, Sorry I missed you. I will return on tomorrow. Merci, Pr. Dunstin."

●●●●●●●●●●●●

Entering Horsed I marvel at the girls and the women covered from head to toe in vivid colors. Red, orange, yellow, lavender, endless solids and splash patterns walking arm-in-arm, their beautiful brown faces and widened eyes peering through the scarf like cameo medallions. Talking and laughing in whispers.

I marvel at the comradeship among the boys who are playing soccer in the middle of the bumpy and dusty road. Many without shoes but it makes no difference. Entering the classroom I hear them with one another. Talking. Listening. Laughing.

The children have each other. Bilal is off to see his soon to be bride. I too desire companionship and before entering the classroom I call Lizette and asked her to join me for drinks.

"I'd love too."

<u>TEN</u>

Thursday, May 31, 2007, 8:39 P.M.

Kempinski, overlooking the water.

"What's on your mind? You seem heavy."

"Aw nothin'."

"Carter, talk to me. Please."

"Well...I've been here since November of last year and I have found nothing of record so far. I've daily been with a man whom I considered a friend and he tells me today that he is getting married the day after tomorrow. I feel left out because he knows his soon to be wife because of me and I haven't even been invited to the wedding. I had one friend, a very special friend, that I lost a few days after meeting you, and since then something inside me has gotten lost as well. I've got connections here that are no more than functional. No real relationships. Sometimes I feel like I'm just functioning without purpose because my passion is slipping away. No one really misses me back in the States except for my mom and my sister. Them's my girls. And in my mind I can't stop hearing the words of my ex-wife who constantly reminded me that I had become boring. She also thinks that I am in Africa looking for gold and telling everyone otherwise but that's another story. 'Perfunctory' she called me. And another thing, I…"

"Shhh." She touches her index finger to my lips. "Look around you."

"Yes, the resort is beautiful but…"

"Shhh. Look around you. The Horn of Africa is incredible and most of the world knows nothing of it. The Gulf of Aden is absolutely amazing with the shimmer of the moon dancing on its surface. The breeze at night balances the stifling heat by day to perfection. Sadly, you are so entangled in your party of pity that you are missing the fact that the lady in your presence desires to know you better."

"Waiter, check please!"

We exit the front door of the resort. Hand in hand. Parked near the entrance is a black Mercedes with tinted windows and a yellow smiley face sticker on the right rear window. It could be the same car that we saw earlier today, but I've got other things on my mind.

Cultivating meaningful relationships has not been one of my stronger character traits and before meeting Lizette I had accepted two considerations. One, I will succeed. Two, no one will be there to share in my success. Such thinking has allowed me to concentrate on professional achievements, but Lizette has awakened in me the idea that all of the world's accolades mean nothing if there is no one special to share the moment.

Her beauty cannot go unnoticed but what strikes me about her is an inner quality that touches me deeply and fills me with the hope that the right one for me has been found and I am finally ready to appreciate the same. She doesn't simply occupy a space to relieve my loneliness, she captivates my imagination and moves me to desire a brighter tomorrow with a woman who will support me and know that I will do the same for her.

Resistance is futile and tonight I am choosing to give into love. I've held her, hugged her, tasted her lips and massaged her soft and tender body. The desire and the intensity is there and though we have not, neither of us feels deprived.

Everything about her does something for me. Her laugh. Her touch. Her spirit. Tonight, I am choosing to give into love.

James Taylor said it best, *"There's something in the way she moves."*

Case in point, instead of walking to her flat, we stroll.

<u>ELEVEN</u>

Friday, June 1, 2007, 8:15 A.M.

I am roused by the ringing of my phone.

I roll out of bed sporting only my boxers and I reach for my watch which is on the nightstand. "Its 8:15, who could this be?"

I stumble to the living room as the phone continues to announce its presence on the floor, under a chair, lying next to my trousers.

"Hello."

"*Bonjour,* Professeur Dunstin, I got your note yesterday. What time shall I expect you?"

"Good morning, Professor Dublé. I think I will have to pass on coming to the lab today. I plan to go over my notes to see if changes of approach are needed."

Lizette walks into the room and comes up behind me. She opens her white silk robe, which compliment her white silk bra and lady boxers. She presses her warm body against mine. She wraps her arms around my waist and gently moves her hands up to my chest. She tenderly massages. I feel the softness of her hair between my shoulder blades as she leans against me. Her scent…

"I'm sorry Professor, but I would definitely like to come in tomorrow if it's convenient?"

"I will be here early to grade papers."

"I will see you then."

"*Au revoir.*" The phone falls on the floor.

I turn and put my hands on her tiny waist. I will admit that the image of my calloused brown hands on her soft and creamy brown skin turns me on. With these hands, I trace her facial lines arriving at her lips so delicate. We kiss. With these hands, I stroke her silky black hair which lays lazily over her shoulders. We kiss. With these hands, I slowly move down her arms, reaching her hands, bringing them to my mouth. I kiss her palms. We reach for one another's face, lips locked. Eyes fixed. Passionate. Intense. Warm embrace. Nice, very very nice.

I sit on the bar stool and watch as she goes into the kitchen.

"What would you like for breakfast Professeur Carter Dunstin love on my life sexy man?"

"First I'd better ask, you luscious Cape Verde vixen who has forced my nose wide open, can you cook?" Smiles.

"You'll soon find out. Now, what would you like?"

"Whatever you cook is fine with me."

"I overheard that you plan to use today as a 're-focusing' day."

"Well, yes and no. I'd like to spend most of the day with you if that's possible, but later I do plan to go to the room and look over my notes to make sure that I am on the right track."

She smiles and kisses me on the forehead, "I will always make time for you." She turns on the burner.

Another thing I had to ask, "So how was that possible?"

"What's that *ma cheri*?"

"What happened last night?"

"Last night you were wonderful."

"Don't get me wrong, I really enjoyed being with you. The touching and the being together was wonderful. The talking and laughing was truly different. Last night was amazing but how is it that we didn't…you know…do it."

She comes around the bar and stands between my legs while I sit on the stool. She leans towards me and wraps her arms around my waist, playing coy, "Do what?"

"You know…it."

"That's *why* you were so wonderful. You knew I wasn't ready, and you allowed me to dictate the terms of our encounter. You were aggressive, yet gentle all in one. Carter Dunstin, I find you irresistible and quite special. You are everything that I have dreamed of in a man. I'm lucky to have you in my life."

She kisses me on the cheek and returns to the stove. "Scrambled or over easy?"

"Scrambled. Do you mind if I do some work while I'm here?"

"Not if you don't mind if I do the same?"

"Agreed."

We eat. She's an excellent cook.

We work. She in the bedroom, and me at the living room table. We each get a lot accomplished and it was gratifying to know that someone was there who really cared for me and that I really cared for as well.

Though the day was productive the gentle touching, the unmerited kisses, and the intermittent embraces made it ever so special.

The choice to love seems to work best when it involves the right person and for me, Lizette is the one.

I think the word is, "smitten."

<u>TWELVE</u>

Saturday, June 2, 2007, 7:30 A.M.

Warm shower. Shared. Nice.

I look in the mirror after having brushed my teeth. "New day." I feel renewed and energized, loving Djibouti all over again. Optimistic in ways never imagined. Yesterday Lizette washed my clothes, and as I dress I think of how I get to wear the thoughtfulness of her care for the rest of the day.

I go to the living room and I reach down to pick up my backpack only to stand and look into the eyes of the woman that's has captured my heart. Thick bath robe. The sight of her weakens and emboldens me at the same time. Perplexing, this love thing.

We embrace. "What's on your agenda for today?"

"8:30 this morning I have to meet with a Kuwaiti client to close on a land acquisition deal. I'll bring the paperwork home to complete and after that I'll be sitting here waiting for your call. Ready to prepare you the best dinner of your life. Can I cook? ."

The morning sunlight peers through the blinds and gently highlights her softly beautiful brown eyes. Cape Verdeans are generally considered a molatto people. The island was a haven for the slave trade to the United States and the Caribbean. Her creamy brown skin, her wet and silky black hair, even her stature speaks well of her heritage. Her personal drive and business acumen speak well of her personality and purpose. I now realize how hard it is hard to leave someone so beautiful and so right for me. "Hey babe, remind me to tell you about a special friend of mine that was killed a few months ago."

I'm off to the Université with Disney's *"Song of the South"* and the voice of James Baskett running through my mind, *"Zip-a-Dee-Doo-Dah, Zip-a-Dee-ah, My oh my, what wonderful day."* This morning is cooler than normal and I feel fantastic. The school's only about four miles away so I begin walking.

I dial. "Hey sweetie, thank you, for being that spark that I was missing in my life."

"No. Thank you Carter, you are perfect combination of nice and nasty…and I love it."

•••••••••••

Reaching the Université, I was surprised my swollen ego made it through the door. She called me, "nice-nasty." Oh yeah.

THIRTEEN

Saturday, June 2, 2007, 8:45 A.M.

"Good morning, Professeur Dublè."

He appears busy. Dismissive. "Good morning, Professeur Dunstin, I'm sure you have business to attend to so please close the door behind you when you leave." I get the impression that my not coming to the lab on yesterday didn't agree with him but I had the best night of any person on the Continent so I care little for his bitchiness. I close the door on my way across the hall to the Zone.

Lab coat, check. Mask, check. A530, check. Cassette tape recorder, check. Backpack opened. Notebook and *BIC*s, always. I survey the room and conclude that nothing has been altered. Continuity is extremely important when conducting research. Headphones on. Nano on. It's time for research!

"Ladies and gentleman, the first mentally stimulating musical selection of the day will be coming from the one, the only, Bootsy Collins! *'Yabbadabbadusi Baba Bootzilla here...'*"

A530 set on video. Blank cassette rotating. Record. I narrate, "I am at the Université de Djibouti. The time is now 9:17 A.M. The date is Saturday, June 2, 2007. The contents of the glass examination enclosure have been in place since Thursday, May 31, 2007, at around 7 P.M. Approximately 38 hours. I am removing the black cloth that has covered the enclosure and…oh my goodness."

I want to shout and puke at the same time. All I could manage is, "Oh my goodness."

The enclosure is filled with hundreds of larvae. Hundreds! It is the most stupendously disgusting sight I have ever seen in my life.

I continue documenting my observations detailing how the maggots are brownish white and are completely covering the chicken. Hundreds! Each approximately 6mm in length. Separate they are maggots but combined they form a formidable blanket of attacking brownish white undulations. Their movements and their numbers are amazing to watch.

There are seventeen adult flies in the dome. I lure one into the examination portal. It is immobilized using a spray form of dry ice. The purpose is to freeze the sample without killing it. I quickly begin the examination using the magnifying class and notating any immediate oddities or characteristics. In size it is much bigger than the average American housefly, but there are almost 120,000 known and classified members of the Order, Diptera, Class, Insecta and Phylum, Anthropoda. This one fly has a lot of cousins which makes it difficult to determine what is considered normal. Some of my colleagues have estimated that almost 250,000 to 750,000 insects in this order, class and phylum are yet to be found, identified and classified. The Order called Diptera includes flies, mosquitoes, midges, gnats, and others and though they have their place in the "circle of life" they are also the most dangerous carriers of diseases which ultimately lead to death. More human suffering and has been attributed to germs carried by members of the Order Diptera than any other creature.

I photograph the specimen. Frontal. Sides. Rear. Top. Bottom. Close, and closer than close. It begins to move, so I quickly return it to the portal and into the enclosure. It drops in, no harm done. It begins to stir and stands upright but within seconds, two of its adult family members fly toward it and immediately begin biting its wings. Awake, it is now immobilized by betrayal and the examined fly is devoured within two minutes. This manner of attack suggest a veracious appetite marked by a lack of communal allegiance. Survival 101. Two flies initiate the attack, but six help to carry out the death sentence. I quickly switch the camera back to video mode and capture the event. Incredible.

After hours of observation and note taking I go through the taxonomist journals to find more information on this peculiar looking specimen. I find nothing.

Using the computer I try matching this it with anything previously listed. Nothing.

Knowing that this the process of research and verification is usually rather lengthy, I elicit the help of the students back at Clarkmore. I email the pictures with corresponding notations to Dr. James Heggie, Chair of the Biology Department. His task is to take the forwarded information and give it to graduate research students who are eager to take part in the project. The videos are too large to send electronically, and I actually don't want to give everything away until I have some sense of what I have found. For now, the pictures and notes will do.

•••••••••••

Time flies.

I go to Dublé's office and find him sitting at his desk, glasses to the tip of his nose, grading papers. I knock.

He never lifts his head but responds, "Yes."

I'm a bit irritated because I have to talk to the top of his balding white head but I continue with this foolish game, "Excuse me Professor, how long do you plan to be here today?"

"I must finish these papers. I will be here for awhile."

Feeling awkward, "Thank you. Late start. Gotta keep working, you know." I turn to walk away.

He calls out, "Professeur Dunstin." Feeling like a kid in the Principal's Office, I stop and turn around while he continues, "Professional courtesy is always extended to any colleague, but personally I find your dealings with Mademoiselle Moniette a bit disturbing after I specifically asked you to leave her strictly alone."

I was not prepared for his petty little comment. My initial feeling of excitement was soon replaced by my disappointment in Dublé. "To make such a statement my friend, at least have the dignity to look me eye to eye. I would try to defend your comment but I cannot. Though I, nor she, planned our initial meeting we have become rather close over time. Very close. With that said, I frankly don't see how my dealings with Mademoiselle Moniette should be of any concern to you and I hope it won't interfere with on professional relationship." I am sure that I failed to hide my displeasure to his line of questioning. He says nothing.

Back to the Zone. More pictures, cassette tapes and notes.

•••••••••••••

Standing in the hallway. I dial. "Hello Bilal…I just called to say congratulations on your wedding today."

“Thank you Professeur. I am most happy.”

“You should be happy. You’re a good man and you deserve it. May peace and success be your friend.”

“*Shukran.*”

“*Afwan.*”

•••••••••••

Two more hours of research and documentation. The information concerning today’s revelations and progress I have saved on a thumb drive that I place in my pocket. I leave my backpack and all other relevant items in the room with the understanding that I will be returning early in the morning. The door is secured. Lights out.

Dublé is not in his office. I leave a note. “Pr. Dublé, Merci. Pr. Dunstin.”

I call for a taxi. I depart.

•••••••••••

It is time to celebrate today’s possibilities. I call Lizette, “Sorry so late Sweetie. Meet me at Kempinski. Twenty minutes.”

“Dinner is waiting right here. Come to me.”

“Got Merlot?”

FOURTEEN

Saturday, June 2, 2007, 8:31 P.M.

I exit the taxi. "Keep the change."

Walking to Lizette's flat, I jump out of the way of a speeding black Mercedes, tinted windows…smiley! My relaxed pace turns into an all-out sprint! Something is not right!

I reach her apartment. "Damn!"

Her door has been kicked in. I enter. There are signs of a struggle. Table knocked over, lamp still lit but on the floor, chairs on their side. The meal she'd prepared had been dumped in the trash. I check the rooms. No Lizette.

I sit briefly on the couch praying and thinking.

I recall the words of Professeur Dublé, "a troubled woman to be avoided."

I dial hoping that he might be able to shed some light on his assertions. "Professeur Dublé something has happened and I…?"

"Dunstin, are you hurt?"

"No but Lizette may be in serious danger."

"I warned you about her. Where are you now?"

"I'm at her flat, across from the Kempinski. The Chartres. Apartment 12. "

"Stay put! I am on my way. I will call when I get in the area."

My mind wonders. "What can she be involved in?"

In the distance, I hear the rare sound of sirens. I am encouraged. "The police."

Just then, a dark green van pulls up. Screeeech! The side door opens revealing a man with a gun pointed at the head of Bilal who is tied up, gagged and lying on his side. "Get in!"

Entering the van, I hear the sound of the sirens going in the opposite direction.

I am struck on the back of the head and the next thing I hear is sound of my head bouncing off the floor of the van. *Thunk*!

Lights out.

FIFTEEN

Saturday, June 2, 2007, 11:11 P.M.

Time elapsed, I don't know. When I awaken I am laying on my side with both hands tied securely behind my back. My legs are also tied. The burlap bag that was placed over my head is removed. I gasp for air, sweating profusely. Vision lazily shifting from cloudy to clear.

The room is dimly lit. It appears to be a warehouse. Various items, food and sundry supplies are stacked on pallets.

Bilal is tied up and seated in a chair to my left about six feet away. His right eye is swollen and he is bloodied about the forehead.

A man comes from behind and picks me up then places me in a chair next to Bilal.

Between us stands a well manicured African man with a gun. His fingernails are polished, clear coated. His blue pants are carefully ironed along with his yellow short sleeve shirt. His shoes are polished, well heeled, not the normal worn out look of the average local. He is talking to another man that I do not see in the room. They are speaking a mixture of Arabic and Somaleeze. I cannot understand.

"Bilal, are you alright?" The man walks over and begins twisting my ear. "Aghhh!"

"Shush!" he then wraps me on the head with a ruler. I've seen this man before, he is one of the twins we saw at Lac Assal last Thursday. He speaks and Bilal translates.

"Professeur, he says that we have offended their operation. They have been conducting the business of exporting from Lac Assal for a long time. He says they do good business and somehow we have offended the family of Na'im. They no longer want us to return and it is becoming a tribal conflict. The warlords in the Afar region are not happy."

The other brother comes from around the stacked bags of wheat. He begins talking through Bilal.

"We are not sure who you are working for, but we know that you are connected with the government. This is a one time deal. Walk away with no more hurt. Stay away from Lac Assal. Leave Djibouti."

The brother between us slowly pours water over my head. As a few drops reach my mouth they mingle with the dried crimson, the taste of blood. The blow to the head left me opened.

"I mean you no disrespect. I am only a scientist. I am here to conduct research on insects. I mean you no disrespect. I am not in the exporting business. I am no threat. I only wish to continue my research at Lac Assal." Bilal translates.

The response, "Do you think we are fools?" I am then hit on the head with the ruler.

"Hey man, I'm telling the truth! Bilal can you explain this to them."

"I have tried Professeur. They will not listen."

Smack! He hits Bilal with the ruler before he can utter another word.

I have nothing to lose, "Where's the girl?"

He smacks me on the head with the ruler, "What girl?"

"Look man, you know what girl I'm talking about and if you hit me with that damn ruler one more time..." *Thunk*. The sound of my head bouncing off the warehouse floor.

Lights out.

SIXTEEN

Sunday, June 3, 2007, 6:10 A.M.

Bilal and I are throw violently around the back of the van as the driving seems to take pleasure in swerving and exploiting potholes. I am bound with the burlap bag on my head. Even now the questions loom, "What the hell have I done to get to this point? I am a scientist, this makes no sense at all."

While still on a bumpy course the side door opens. The burlap is no match for the foul and wretched sting of death that is invading my nostrils. I clearly hear the words, "You tell and the girl dies! You stay in Africa and you die!" With that, I am pushed out of the moving vehicle.

I hit the ground hard, the sand and the rocks stripping my flesh. I soon roll to a stop against a pile of *something*. The smell is intense. Extreme stank is the only way to describe it. I struggle to get the bag off of my head by rubbing it on the ground. The smell is unbearable and I have to work hard to contain the feeling of panic beginning to rise. I frantically work to get the burlap bag off my head which is now hindering my ability to breathe in the funk that I don't want to smell anyway. Damn. I begin gasping while struggling. The bag loosens and I am overtaken by a barrage of smells that are combining to create intense agitation. Breathing deeply to avoid suffocation I take in more of the stank.

Daylight is breaking and now that the bag is off, I wish I were still blinded…I now see that have landed on a mound of animal carcasses.

In my old world of "optimism and innocence" the morning light usually brought with it the hope of new opportunities and possibilities. Now, all I see is death. Piles of death. Cows. Bulls. All grouped according to color. I landed on a pile of white bulls. Some dried and rotted, like jerky. Some are swollen and are ready for the African sun in cooperation with flesh eating insects and intestinal bacteria to provide an exit for the expanding gastric acids. Some are skeletons. The stage of decomposition matters very little right now. Old death. New death. It's all death and I'm laying on a pile of it. Damn!

To put it plainly, this is way beyond disgusting.

I look around for Bilal and I want to call out to him but the stank has gotten in my mouth. Gagging. Up my nose. So many flies…overwhelming!

I manage, "Bilal, where are you?."

His response is equally and understandably weak, "Here Professeur." I see him about twenty feet away from me.

Struggling to get free I use more energy, requiring heavier breathing, increasing the choking and gagging reflex. Bilal seems to be experiencing the same. We both struggle to free ourselves for about two or three minutes, it seemed like hours.

Hopelessness, danced in and out of my mind and it dawns on me that I have no song. Usually, there's a song or a rhythm either playing in my ear or playing in my mind that generally fits any given situation or to set set a certain mood. Much like a reality soundtrack to carry me through life changes, but at this extreme moment when I needed it most, I had no song. Empty.

Thinking back, I've not had a song since last night when they hit me in the back of the head. Music, since I was a child, has brought clarity and insight to the various stages of my life and now, when it might be helpful, I can't hear the music. None in my head. None in my heart. None in my soul. My inner soundtrack is on mute and this is allowing for thoughts of doubt and despair to take advantage of this dire situation. Optimism is dormant. Death is all around and it is beginning to creep in. I don't know what I had done to deserve this but at this critical moment all of my energies are needed to fight the overwhelming desire to quit.

I am on my back and looking toward the sky. I notice the early morning collections of buzzards and several other birds looking for breakfast. They spiral, wings outstretched, riding the thermal current. Thought their presence doesn't help the situation, their effortless movement take me to an immediate, yet temporary, place of peace..

"Professeur, come to me. We must help each other."

"Good idea." Like inchworms we begin scootching toward one another. Over the bones and rocks. Over the sinew and sand. Skin and hair chunks. "Just get to Bilal. Just keep moving!"

Exhausted, we reach one another. The place of our meeting was directly in front of one of the foulest smelling mounds of death. We turn and place ourselves back to back, trying to remove each other's ropes. Silence. We were in the midst of freshly dead bovine, brown cows to be exact. They lay there with their feet up, and their stomachs bloated and ready to explode when the noonday heat arrives. Their eyes glossed over while flies and gnats are enjoying their oozing juices. Teeth protruding. Beetles partaking of the buffet. I had rolled from dried dead to new dead. The major change was the intensity of the stank and the attending insects.

Here again, the minutes felt like hours but we managed to loosen each other's ropes which was not easy considering our limbs were numb from being bound overnight. Freed, we attempt to stand but aren't able. The feeling of circulation hadn't returned. My shoulders and arms were sore from the awkward positioning and the painful rolling and sliding that occurred during our unconventional method of disembarking.

Free. Hardly. We were loosed but unable to move with purpose. Stumbling when trying to stand we fall back onto the waiting pile of life's last element. Decomposition.

Little things come to mind as I begin to take inventory. My watch is still on my wrist. I reach in my pocket and find my wallet, cell phone, thumbdrive and my keys. I think, "Robbery was not their motive." I try to make a phone call but there is no reception. Our clothing is torn. We are bleeding from our elbows, shoulders and knees. Each of us is missing a shoe.

After about ten minutes, sensation returning. We recover our missing shoes. We can't cover our nose with our shirts because we are completely saturated with the nastiness. The decay and disease is attacking us from every direction and to compound our precarious disposition, Bilal points to a pack of about twenty wild dogs that are cautiously coming to investigate our presence. We hurl bones to ward them away. They lurk, maintaining a safe distance.

I look to Bilal and give the universal sign of "Which way?" Both of us are trying to avoid a mouthful of awful, he doesn't speak but starts in a northward direction. We walk.

After about six hundred yards or so, the stank begins to lessen. Slightly. Continuing on, we see a small house complete with white fence. Most of the houses outside of town are shanties and shacks made with large pieces of any scrap available, but this house was well constructed. Intentional. It was painted white and had a black slanted roof.

There are three kids kicking a soccer ball in the yard. Decay, disease and death are very much all around and these kids are enjoying a game of *kurat al-qadam.*

We approach. The kids run toward us giving the universal extended hand, which is the sign for water.

"No."

Noticing our general presentation they turn and run to the front door of the house, "*Abba! Abba!*" The father appears. Bilal walks toward him and they talk.

I sit near the fence and try to make sense of the last twelve hours. Lizette's door. Her apartment. The warehouse. Being accused of taking something. It dawns on me that Bilal was apparently taken and beaten on his wedding day. Damn.

Returning from the house, Bilal reports that, "We can use their cleaning water in the back, but do not drink." The water was cloudy to start, after we washed the nastiness from our faces and arms, the water took on the appearance of mud and blood. The smell remained but the relief was much appreciated.

The kids kick the ball our way. We kick it back. We continue kicking the ball back and forth for a few minutes. The change of pace and purpose did us good. The momentary smiles are invaluable.

One of the kids picks up a stick and hurls it in the distance. The waiting dogs begin to scatter as the kids take chase.

The smell. The heat. The atmosphere. Nothing changes, but I find it remarkable that the children are being raised near a field of putrefaction. The repercussions can be devastating to their health yet they live their lives. They are playing and kicking a ball. No worries. Humans throughout civilization have constantly shown the ability to adapt and overcome. This place of comfort in the middle of discomfort is the metaphor I need to get back on track.

I too, must adapt and overcome.

I am encouraged.

Vomiting and weakened but moving on. The more we walk the pungency lessens. There were still smells to be tolerated but I believe the worst is behind us. Continuing on, I realize that the worst is still on us.

"Where are we?"

"According to the caretaker back at the house, we are directly between the border of Somalia and the southern edge of Camp LeMonier. Eight kilometers in either direction. That way."

The conversing ends. We walk. We've gone from animal remains and are now walking through trash and refuse. Not as tangy to the nostrils. There are people combing through the trash hoping to find usable items. A bull dozier moves the heaps while people steer clear. Looking around we are standing in the middle of five hundred yards of trash in either direction. I see the smoke from the incinerator in the distance and it enters my mind that it might need to speed up its operation. It might be a little behind…just a little.

We reach the main road and join the daily trek of sojourners. Ladies with baskets on their heads, perfect balance. Men carrying containers of oil. Trucks passing by that are overcrowded with those who ride to Djibouti City everyday from the outer regions and the hills of Somalia. We walk.

My black skin serves me well as I blend with the others. I too, am a sojourner. At 6' 1" I am taller than the rest and I am a bit larger than the average Djiboutian, but at this very moment in time I am a sojourner and more than anything else, I am African. Differences fade. Bilal says nothing and I notice the pride in his walk. I say nothing, drawing strength from his demeanor. Walking among the others, I may not be mistaken as Djiboutian but at this very moment I feel the presence of my ancestors who are seated in the balconies of eternity and are encouraging my wearied soul. Step by step I am encouraged. I draw strength from those around me and from the sun. At this very moment I am fully African.

Passing Douda village, I see Camp LeMonier.

<u>SEVENTEEN</u>

Sunday, June 3, 2007, 7:20 A.M.

We reach the main entrance of the base and are stopped by the Marines of the 6th Provisional Security Company who are tasked with the responsibility of securing the perimeter and in triple digit temperatures they stand alert and at the ready in full battle armour including Kevlar and sappy plates. I am convinced that our aroma preceded our arrival but they remained respectful and professional.

I present my Military ID and Bilal presents his Camp LeMonier ID, having served as a guide for base excursions with the MWR. We are waved forward and are instructed to place all pocketed items and all jewelry in the plastic container. Cell phone, thumbdrive, keys, wallet, money. Removing my watch, I am reminded of our ordeal as I remove a clump of animal fur stuck in the clasp joined together by a chunk of decaying meat. "That's nasty."

Sergeant Kirkendohl gives instruction, "Gentlemen, please standby." In front of us are Corporal Lounds and Lance Corporal Hohman. They never flinch but willingly step aside for Privates Flath and Alexander to perform the pat-down search.

Undescribable fumes are stirred as the rubber-gloved Marines tend to their business.

Search complete, the Sergeant returns from the office having made a phone call. He returns our ID's. "You may place your items back into your pockets." When doing so, I look at my phone and notice that I haven't missed any calls. I hope Lizette is okay.

"Gentleman, come with me."

"Thank you Sergeant."

Walking away from the gate, we hear a collective, "DAMMMNNNN!" Now, I feel safe. For a moment there I was getting self-conscious.

We are escorted to the Quarterdeck. "Both of you are to remain here."

"Thank you Sergeant."

Moments later we are introduced to Master Sergeant Moore. She works in the Admiral's Office. "Gentlemen, I will be assisting you to conduct your business but before we go any further we must get you cleaned up. Sergeant Kirkendohl, get both of these men to the showers. Now!"

"Master Sergeant, what about the Djiboutian?"

"What part of '*both*' do you not understand?! I need *BOTH* of these men cleaned up and given a change of clothing. Make it happen! Then get them to the Medics and to my office. ASAP."

"Yes, Master Sergeant." He quickly secures a trash bag for each of us and escorts us to the donation clothing closet. We find what we need to replace what we have. We secure towels and soap from the Emergency Medical Unit and are speedily taken to the shower point.

The warm water irritated the open cuts and scratches on my marred flesh, not to mention the open wounds on the back of my head. Body aches and tenderness. After five minutes of scrubbing and allowing the flow to massage my back, the smell begins to disappear. After ten minutes of the same, clean never felt so good.

Dressed in shorts, t-shirts and flip flops, we are escorted to the EMU for a check-up, stitches, and tetanus shots. I hate needles. Bilal fainted.

We exit the building looking like two wounded warriors on vacation. Bilal has an icepack over his right eye which is swollen shut and ten stitches were used to close the gash on his left temple. Three stitches for the cut on his right cheek.

For me, sixteen stitches to the back of the head for the first blow and twelve stitches for the second, a diagnosed concussion and a bottle of aspirin for the road. Extra bandages for both of us.

We are then escorted to Master Sergeant Moore's office. "Outstanding Sergeant Kirkendohl, I'll take it from here but I want you to stand by." She picks up the phone, "Sir, they are ready."

Hanging up, she asks, "Are either of you hungry?"

Considering what we just walked through, I almost threw-up just thinking about the answer. "No ma'am."

"Both of you are going to be interviewed concerning your recent incident. It will behoove each of for you to answer the questions honestly and completely. We trackin'?"

"Yes ma'am."

"Do you see any bars on my collar? No you do not! That's Master Sergeant Moore! Got it?"

Bilal and I are a bit intimidated and in unison we slowly respond, "Yes Master Sergeant…ma'am."

"Okay gentleman let's get going."

Bilal sheepishly raises his hand, "Master Sergeant."

"Speak."

"What is *behoove*?"

<u>EIGHTEEN</u>

Sunday, June 3, 2007, 9:42 A.M.

We arrive at Camp LeMonier's Enduring Freedom Chapel where the Worship Service has started.

"Bilal, are you going to be comfortable here?"

"Professeur, I would much prefer to offer *qaḍâ*. To make up for missed prayer."

"Sergeant Kirkendohl escort Bilal to one of the Muslim vendors at the Commissary. I'm sure one of them will ensure that he is given a prayer rug and a bottle of water for cleansing. When he is finish meet us in the Chaplain's Office."

"Yes Mass-Sergeant."

Master Sergeant Moore and I slip into the back of the Chapel while Chaplain McCreary is completing his sermon. "Each of us must surrender. *Never* to surrender to another man, but to surrender your heart, mind and soul to the One who created us all. Only then, can *true* victory be attained. Let us pray…"

Amen.

I am taken to the Chaplain's Office after the service. I sit for a few moments. Alone. Reflecting.

Bilal arrives.

Whispers. "I believe them."

"You believe what Professeur?"

"I believe that they will kill Lizette if we tell anyone what really happened."

"I agree."

"Where is the Mitsu?"

"At my home. They took me while I was returning from walking some well-wishers down the road."

"Okay, so I will say that we had returned from Lac Assal and that we stopped by your house, and we were made to get in the green van. They wanted to rob us but we had nothing to give them. Then we were hit in the head and knocked out. There were five men. They tied us up, put bags over our heads and dropped us in the animal dump this morning. We walked here. We won't mention the warehouse. No detailed descriptions, other than the green van. Agreed?"

"Agreed." After a brief silence he asks, "You are aware that they delivered us to the land of the dead for a reason?"

"Yes, and I intend to find what that reason is."

Chaplain McCreary enters, followed by Ambassador Singleton and an NCIS Agent named Brokenbow. After formal introductions they ask us to explain how we came to arrive at Camp LeMonier in our most recent condition. I explain without deviating from the recently devised script. Bilal says nothing.

Chaplain McCreary listened and gives us a look of empathy as if to understand how we are feeling.

Ambassador Singleton remains stoic. Straight faced. He sits with leg crossed. Cool.

Agent Brokenbow guided the inquiry, "Help me to understand. They were trying to rob you…of what?"

"We don't know. As a scientist, all I carry are tools for on-site investigation and examination and we return with specimen for further examination. Yesterday we returned with nothing."

"You've been researching in Lac Assal for about eight months now?"

"Seven, actually."

"Have you had problems with anyone up to this point?"

"No sir."

"Do you owe anyone money?"

"No sir."

Brokenbow slows his cadence and speaks louder to Bilal as if he were deaf and illiterate.

"Have…you…had…any…problems…with…anyone?"

Bilal glances towards me then answers with the same cadence. "No…sir."

"Do…you…like…Professor…Dunstin?"

Bilal responds, "He…is…my…brother."

The comment catches me off-guard but I quickly clarify, "Figuratively speaking."

After an hour of Q & A the Chaplain clearly appeared to be disinterested, the Ambassador remained unreadable and having made no progress, Agent Brokenbow stopped and said, "Thank you Gentlemen, that'll be all for now." We stand and shake hands.

The Ambassador pulls me close and whispers, "Professor, this could be classified as an incident. I don't like incidents. From now on, you are to call me, or my office every evening. Got it."

"Yes Ambassador."

The Chaplain remarks, "I'll see you next Sunday. Worship Service starts at 9."

"I'll do what I can Chaplain."

Brokenbow chimed in, "Tomorrow I will accompany you to your site at Lac Assal."

Thinking of the threat to Lizette, "Actually, the events since yesterday have left me uneasy. I don't think I'll be returning for a few days. I need to re-evaluate. I'll keep you posted."

He hands me his business card and continues, "Each of you

should have your personal items? I'll need to keep your clothing for further examination."

The Ambassador remarks, "Professor, this Wednesday I return to the States as I do every six months. Be sure to contact me, or my office daily. Come by the Embassy if you need anything."

"Thank you Ambassador. Will do."

The meeting ends and NCIS Agents Rhoden and Mayhew drive us to our respective homes. First to Bilal's house. Luckily, Numa is at the home of her family awaiting word from her recently vacant and newly disfigured husband. His disappearance on the day of his wedding will only magnify the altered condition of his current appearance. He's in trouble. Neighbors gather.

The show of community concern aided Agent Rhoden who conducts inquiries. "Did you see who might have taken your friend from his home?" "What color was the vehicle?" "What time was he taken?" Most are reluctant to answer and no one says anything to refute our story.

Agent Mayhew takes pictures of the location. They search the Mitsu. His home. More pictures.

Bilal remarks to the agents, "If the vehicle is clear, I must go and collect my bride. Tomorrow Professeur?"

"No Bilal, not tomorrow. You get some rest. *As-salaamu alaikum.*"

"*Wa 'alaikum as-salaam wa-raHumat ulaahi wa barakaatuh.*"

"What does that mean?"

"It literally means, 'And peace is upon you too, as well as God's mercy and his blessings.'"

For the first time Bilal and I shake hands and embrace. "My brother."

••••••••••••

We arrive at the Menelik and the Agents question the front desk personnel.

They search my room. Finger prints and pictures are taken while I sit in the corner and review my notes and journals. I turn on the laptop and insert the thumb drive. It still works.

"Professor, we'll be in touch."

"Thank you." They depart.

Dailing. "Bilal, tomorrow after midday prayer. Be here."

"But you said…"

"Never mind what I said, we don't have much time and we must find out what is going on, or what we have fallen into. These men know where we live and where we work. We'll never be safe and we need answers. I won't stop until I find Lizette. I owe her that much. Can you be here tomorrow after midday prayer?"

104

"I don't know Professeur, I just…"

"Bilal we don't have much time. I need your help. I have no one else to rely upon but you."

Hesitation. "Yes Professeur. Tomorrow after *al-zuhr*."

I hang up the phone and begin searching the laptop for the right music for the moment. Thinking of Lizette, Eric Clapton understands my plight. If I could *"Change the World."* she would be here with me. Safe.

I open one of the many notebooks stacked on the table, WHEN I FIND WHAT ISN'T, IT WILL BE! Blue *BIC* in hand, I begin recounting recent events.

"Were there cues?"

"Was something said that might have lead to this mess of a situation?"

"What are we accused of stealing?"

I sit and think and write for an hour until my aches and discomfort dominate. I close the notebook and go to the bathroom to get a couple aspirin.

Closing the medicine cabinet, I stand in the mirror and look at my facial scratches and discolorations. Unraveling the bandage and using a hand mirror I look at the wounds on the back of my head. Patches of hair shaved to accommodate the stitches. I delicately remove my shirt and observe the effects of last twenty-four hours on my body.

I fill the tub with water that is as warm as I can tolerate. My body is rest but my mind is on hyper-drive.

Toweling , I begin laughing, "Only in Africa can you get an Irish-American's prayer for safety, a Euro-American's promise of protection, a Native-American leading the investigation, and each watching over an African-American who has an African-African for a brother."

•••••••••••

Weary and in need of inspiration, I dial. "Hey Mom, I didn't want anything, I just wanted to hear your voice. How's everybody doin'?"

Happy to hear from her baby boy, Mom takes the time to give me the family rundown. "Have you talked to your sister yet because she…" In thirty minutes I am caught up on who's healthy and who's not, who's in need and who's got plenty, who's making good choices and the other folks. The comfort I was seeking is found. She concludes by asking, "So how are you doing?"

"I'm good. Things have changed here recently."

"I hope it's for the better."

"I'll know soon. Well, tell everybody I said 'Hey'. I love you Mom." Optimism restored.

Sleep.

NINETEEN

Monday, June 4, 2007, 9:30 A.M.

My phone rings.

"*As-salaamu alaikum.*"

"*Wa 'alaikum as-salaam..*"

"Professeur, can we get started?"

"Sure, how long will it take you to get here?"

"I'm here now." I look out the window and see Bilal leaning against the Mitsu. Bandaged and ready for business.

"I'll be right down." Hurrying to get dressed reminds me of yesterday's ordeal. My body aches along with a headache, but the eagerness of Bilal to get started lessens my discomfort. Clothes on. Thumb drive. Bottle of aspirin. Down the stairs.

"How are you feeling?"

"I hurt all over. Numa is quite upset. She expressed the desire not to become an early widow. Her father no longer believes that I am only your guide and translator, he has insinuated that we are involved in some bad business. I had to assure her entire family that we have done nothing wrong." He pauses, "We have done nothing wrong. Right?"

"You are correct Bilal, we have done nothing wrong and I will understand if you choose to end our working relationship. On the other hand, I must continue doing what I came here to do."

"Last night, I lay in bed. My new bride is lying next to me. I am scared and I am scarred. My body hurts. But in all of my days I have not experienced such…such…excitement. I woke up early and I looked at my wife and I knew I had to do something so that we can sleep without fear. Where to Professeur?"

"The Université."

●●●●●●●●●●●●

I find Professeur Dublé sitting at his desk. He is shocked when he notices my wounds, accented with the head bandage. He stands and with cane in his left hand he begins to walk toward me. "Professeur Dunstin, what has happened?"

"We can talk about that some other time. Some time ago you warned me about Lizette. Why?"

"Ah, Lizette." He leans against the desk, "I find Lizette Moniette to be very driven. She likes things of beauty. Things that men like us could never give her. We might satisfy a women like her for a moment but like all moments, they end. I know that my evidence is flimsy but I think she is involved with some type of trafficking."

"Trafficking what?"

"Khat."

"Come on Dublé, there is no way that Lizette would be involved in khat trafficking. Besides, it's legal here."

"I once tried to win her favor, so I arrived at her office with flowers in hand. Unannounced. I rounded the corner and found her sealing boxes and placing mailing labels on them. She was clearly startled. I walked over to present the flowers only to find that the boxes were stuffed with khat and the labels read Milwaukee, Wisconsin and Minneapolis, Minnesota. With my own eyes Professeur, I saw the boxes. I saw the khat piled high. I was disgusted. I turned and walked out. Only a low life would deal khat to the other side of the world. After that, I have had no time for Mademoiselle Moniette. I avoid her and I don't want to be bothered with her dealings. I encourage you to do the same."

"I might be in too deep though I don't know how. There was an incident with Bilal and myself. I was thinking that she might have something to do with it."

"If your bruises and bandages are evidence of something gone wrong then I would hope that you have talked to the American authorities?"

"Yes and no. I have talked with the authorities but I didn't tell them the truth. I lied because the men who did this to Bilal and I had promised to kill Lizette if I tell. Let's face it Dublé, khat dealer or not, I can't allow her to get hurt. I really didn't have much to tell the authorities anyway. The men want something that I don't have, and they are willing to kill someone that I care about to get it! Damn. The timing couldn't be worse."

"You don't strike me as a man to fall in love so easily."

"Love? No, I'm talking about my research work here. I think I'm moving in the right direction but now it all seems secondary. I feel responsible for Lizette and I can't concentrate."

"Is there any way I can be of assistance?"

"Yes…continue to answer the phone when I call. I am very grateful Dublé. You're a good friend. *Merci*."

"*Il n'y a pas de quoi*. Remember, I warned you about her. I say go on with your research and leave *her kind* to themselves. Let the authorities handle these matters and walk away. Oh pooh, I find it futile to argue with a scientist who seems to possess a conscience, of all things. Go figure. Be careful, my friend. *Au revoir*."

I leave Dublés office and go to the Zone. An hour passes as I sit and do nothing. I don't lift the cloth to check the specimen. I don't check my notes from the backpack that had been here since Saturday. All I do is sit, and think.

With backpack in hand, I exit the room and lock the door.

•••••••••••

Leaving the building I observe Bilal and other Muslims rendering midday prayers.

Daily I hear the melodious voice of the muezzin calling from the minaret at Al-Masjid to all who believe in Allah. Bilal is kneeling on the *sajjada* that he keeps neatly rolled and placed in the back of the Mitsu. His face, hands, and feet have been washed. Shoes removed and placed side by side. All faithful Muslims humble themselves as they go to God. At a particular time each day, within a particular region, all who believe will stop and pray. That's powerful. He respectfully performs the appropriate *rak'as*. Having started the prayer in a standing position, he is now kneeling and bowing with his face to the ground.

After months of not paying attention to the uniqueness of the culture and the people around me I was finally able to understand the words of the prayer. The first of the Five Pillars of Islam is the Shahada, which basically means that there is no god but God and that Muhammad is the prophet of God. It would be considered the Muslim's profession of faith.

Allahu Akbar (God is most great)

> *Ashadu anna la ilaha illa Allah* (I bear witness there
is no god but God)
>
> *Ashadu anna Muhammadan rasul Allah* (I bear
> witness Muhammad is the prophet of God)
>
> *Haiya 'ala al-Salah* (Come to prayer)
>
> *Haiya 'ala ai-falah* (Come to wellbeing)
>
> *Al-Salah khayrun min al-nawn* (Prayer is better than
sleep)
>
> *Allahu Akbar* (God is most great)
>
> *La ilaha illa Allah* (There is no God, but God)

I generally use Bilal's time of prayer to pause and to check my notes or to review the actions needed to complete my research. Until now, I had been driven by the task of research, nothing else mattered and distractions were not allowed, but today was different. Today the voice from the mosque's minaret was awakening something inside of me. Whether it was the weight of recent events or the uncertainty of what might be next, it became very clear that I needed to talk to my God.

I was raised in the Baptist tradition, but recent events have me feeling unsure of my faith. Uncertain. The feeling that comes, I guess, when a person has abandoned their God and life seems to turn against them. Somewhere in my life I stopped praying, I stopped talking to God and receiving the guidance and protection that I was raised to believe would carry me. I stopped trusting in the Almighty and began thinking that my intellect and imagination alone would open doors. I am doing what I am trained and skilled at doing but I lack that higher connection. I need the guidance and strength that only God can give. I need the balance that only faith can provide. I need peace.

At that moment I recalled my days as a little boy, riding to church with my grandparents on Sunday morning. Sleeping in the pew, I'd be awakened by the inspirational and rhythmic intonations of Pastor T. DeWitt Smith, Jr. That was usually accompanied by unbridled shouts of "Preach" and "Amen" from the congregation. The Deacons would be praying, the Mothers would be swaying and the liberating power of the Spirit held it together. Gospel music accentuating the fellowship. Good news. Good times.

Standing there, next to the Mitsu, a feeling of warmth began to flow through my body. It started at the crown of my head and it rushed evenly down to my feet. It wasn't a notion of euphoria that often leads to an outer display but it was much more substantive, something a bit more personal and empowering. It is as if God is whispering in my ear and saying, "I got you."

Without thought and without planning, I fall down on one knee. "Lord, I don't know what to do. I don't know which way to turn, but thank you for letting me know that everything is going to be all right. Thank you for watching over me, even though I haven't been serving you right. I know that You have been with me and You didn't bring me this far to leave me. I don't know what will happen next but I just believe that everything will be all right. I am turning it all over to You. My recent situation with Bilal. My concerns about Lizette. My research. I am turning it all over to You. In the name of Jesus, guide me and thank You for this feeling of comfort. Amen."

Tears of joy flowed. When I needed it most Someone put a reassuring hand on my shoulder and said, "I got you."

Looking for something undiscovered was my mandate. It was my reason for being in Djibouti. Now, the only thing that mattered was doing what was best for Lizette and Bilal and the rest would take care of itself.

We leave the Université and drive to Lizette's apartment.

•••••••••••

Standing in front of her flat nothing is as I had remembered it. The door, including the frame and the hardware has been replaced. Good as new. There are no signs of previous destruction. I try to peek through the window but the curtains are closed. Nothing. I try to shoulder the door. Nothing.

Bilal asks, "Where to Professeur?"

"Lac Assal."

<u>TWENTY</u>

Monday, June 4, 2007, 2:25 P.M.

We've never arrived at Lac Assal this late in the day. Na'im nor his sons come to greet us. I wonder if it was because of the twins and their threats or maybe it was because of the fact that Bilal and Na'im had a disagreement the last time we were here. With so many unanswered questions the landscape appears more even more desolate. No tourist. No one. It is difficult not to feel like a moving target while walking across the salt basin with the ground crunching under our feet. I don't know who and I don't know from where but I feel strongly that someone is watching us our every move.

I survey the three research Sites and given all that we've endured over the past few days I am surprised that each appears to be intact. There are no obvious signs of specimen contamination nor are the any visible signs of alteration to immediate area. I had prepared myself for the possibility of that my work may have been tampered with, or destroyed. Not today. I unpack the A530, the note book, the *BIC* and begin to document my observations at Sites I and II where the raw chicken in the wire cage still exist. The decay is rapid and much of that is due to daily direct exposure to the sun but it must be determined if this is primarily atmospheric or because of other attacking agents. The question must also be answered if another host would bring different results? Can distinct conclusions be drawn from my processes? There is much to document and examine. Little time.

The shadows begin shifting and I respectfully wait as Bilal performs prayer. He kneels and bows on the *sajjada* with the sunrays hitting him on the left as he faces North toward the Ka'ba Shrine in Mecca.

I begin loading the Mitsu and I can't help but to feel as if the scales are falling away from my eyes concerning Djibouti and Lac Assal. Much of my time as been spent here but I am now able to clearly see the beauty of the landscape of this geographically complex regional. The mountains of splendor. The volcanic rocks gathered above the surface. Various sizes. Black, brown, gray. The glass-like clarity of the water which magnifies the snow colored whiteness of the salt laden lake bottom. The occasional bird, arms outstretched, hovering overhead. After seven months, my eyes are finally open and I can take in the splendor that surrounds me. Eerily serene.

Returning the prayer mat to the trunk, Bilal calls for Na'im. No answer.

●●●●●●●●●●●

We drive. I am heavy with the reality of Lizette missing, and we've been assaulted by men who want something that we don't know we possess. Time is passing. No answers.

Observing the barren landscape, "Tell me all you know about khat."

"The khat? Why?"

"I have no proof but Lizette may be involved in khat distribution and that may be why we are in this situation. Tell me all you know about khat."

"For your sake I hope she is not involved because the khat is very big business. It rules the life of Djibouti. After obtaining our independence from the French in 1977, Abba Hassan Gouled Aptidon, our first President tried to ban the khat and I am told that there were riots and looting. Even death threats.

"The khat is outlawed throughout Africa except for a few pocket areas. We get the khat from Ethiopia, but it is also grown in Somalia. The same green and white plane that we've both seen brings it daily in huge bags. The bags are removed from the plane and placed on the transfer trucks by about twenty to thirty workers. The workers wear blue coverall suits with orange safety vest. The workers blow whistles and make noise as they go through town. 'Clear the road! Clear the road!' It's like a daily procession of royalty. Everyone clears the road because they want the khat. The people worship the khat. It goes to the warehouse and is quickly sorted into small bundles and is then delivered to the street vendors at stands around the city.

"The khat is best and most potent when it is fresh, so the khat stands around the distribution center are the most prized. Delivery is quick and by noontime prayer all of the khat has been distributed and sold and ready to be chewed. The cheapest bundles sell for one American dollar but twenty dollars might be spent by a nobleman or during festive and special occasions like birthdays and weddings.

"Only the man is to chew the khat. The khat is not to be chewed by women. Women can sell it, but only men are supposed to chew it. It used to be for the wealthy only, but now every man has his time."

I wonder aloud, "So far you have told me things I already know and I appreciate it but I need to know what does khat do to you? How does it make you feel?"

"You take the khat and you roll it into a ball and stuff it into your jaw. You chew the khat. Most times the men chew the khat at home, but sometimes they gather and chew together. The khat is very, very bitter and the men have to drink tea that is very sweet or soda drinks to deal with the dry mouth.

"Soon the man will get a very easy feeling inside. Happy and light headed. He get's a 'high' you would say. Later, they get very loud and pushy. Fights occur. That is what you would call 'coming down' I guess. It takes you up to good feelings, down to bad feelings and it leaves you empty. No energy.

"A little of the khat is okay, but too much of the khat can cause a man take money needed to feed the family and chew it up and all he will have to show for it is the black teeth that comes from years of chewing the khat. Now in Djibouti, there are hungry women and children because of men who chew the damn khat and will not work. A little khat is okay but too much khat is very bad."

After a few minutes of silence I ask, "You had khat at your wedding didn't you?"

"Yes. It is customary and good luck for the men of both families to sit with the bridegroom and chew the khat after the wedding."

"Is that why you didn't invite me?"

"Professeur, I see the way you look at the people buying and selling the khat. You always have a look of disgust though you say nothing. I did not want to make you uncomfortable and I did not want to ruin Numa's day."

I willingly admit, "The khat stands remind me of the liquor stores in the black communities in America. Seems like there is one on every corner in certain neighborhoods. People taking their hard earned money just to get a buzz or a high. Liquor, just like khat, turns good men into disappointments. Some drink to excess and become drunkards and at that point their family suffers because they spend all they have to satisfy their drinking desire."

Silence.

He asks, "Your father?"

"No he had other vices, but I've seen enough good men reduced to nothing because of liquor."

Silence.

He adds, "I thank you brother."

After hearing about the khat operation in Djibouti I am even more taken aback by Lizette's participation. Maybe I should follow the advise of my friend Professeur Dublé and, "Leave her alone and turn it over to the authorities. Just walk away."

•••••••••••••

Answering my cell phone, I hear the weakened words of Dublé, "Dunstin get to the Université as soon as possible!"

"Professeur are you alright?" Dial tone.

"Bilal, the Université now!"

120

TWENTY-ONE

Monday, June 4, 2007, 6:18 P.M.

We arrive at the Université and find police cars in the parking lot. I make my way upstairs and find Professor Dublé in his classroom. He is sitting in a chair and leaning on a desk with a wastebasket underneath to catch the flow of blood that is oozing from his nose. Blood having already soiled his shirt, I hand him a box of tissue that is sitting on the desk and he continues to wipe himself clean. He then packs tissue up his nose and leans back in the chair. The sight was rather pitiful.

Someone has assaulted a pale, teetering and gentle man whose body has betrayed him. Though I have never asked how it came to be, Dublé exhibits the evidence of his left side being weakened, as if he has suffered a stroke and I'm sure he offered his attackers little defense.

Two Police Officers are standing in the corner of the room talking.

I say nothing but remain present to offer assistance.

"My samples!" I hurry over to the Zone. I unlock the door and quickly scan the room. No apparent damage. Nothing missing or out of place.

I return to Dublé. "What happened?"

"I will tell you when the room is clear."

Ten minutes pass and the last policeman leaves the room.

"I told them that I was trying to break up a fight between two students."

"Is that what happened?"

"There were two men, but they were not fighting one another. They accosted me and asked questions about your friend, Lizette Moniette. They vowed to do me more harm if I said anything to the authorities."

"What did they look like?"

Dublé hesitates, looks left then right, he appears fearful as he lowers his voice, "Oddly, they were twins. African twins. I have been here for years, but I have never seen twins. A mirror image of one another. Extraordinary."

"What were they asking for?"

"They wanted to know where the money was hiding?"

"Money? What money?"

"Apparently some of her dealings have gone bad. These thugs would rather beat-up on innocent educators than to deal with her and her network."

"What network?" I protest, "This doesn't make sense. These twins already know where she is and they have dealt with her directly. Why do they need to come to you for her affairs? She was kidnapped. The door to her apartment was kicked in. She hasn't returned my calls!"

Dublé tries to stand. I assist by supporting him under his left arm. His cane is in use in his right. Upright, looking disorderly, he gives his opinion, *"Mon ami,* it might be time to consider her kidnapping, a ruse. Heed my warning, Mademoiselle Lizette Moniette is not who you think she is and may never become who you want her to be."

●●●●●●●●●●●●

Eyes wide, I sit on the top step of the stairway. Clarity replaces the mental cloudiness.

"How could I have missed it? There are two men who know the whereabouts of Lizette. The twins. Two men willingly and mercilessly assaulted Bilal and myself. The twins. Two men, the twins, attacked Professeur Dublé. The killers of Maxi, Alqaanoon and Rashaaqa. Law and Grace...gotta be the same.

The twins. The monsters that beat and killed my Lil' Buddy have basically worked to destroy everyone that is important to me. The twins. The damn twins!"

Head in hands, I imagine the blows rendered upon Maxi. The business-like brutality of his mirrored attackers. The blows to the face. The feet stomping. The blood pooling. He clutched the backpack. I envision the pushing, the shoving, the beating given to Dublé. A good friend. I cease imagining when considering the disrespect and the probable violation of Lizette. Is she still alive? *"Why is this happening? What have I done?"*

Weakness emerges and tears begin to puddle, *"Oh hell no! This ain't time for crying! I got too much thinking, plotting and planning to do. Where do I start? Who cares. Merlot."*

TWENTY-TWO

Monday, June 4, 2007, 8:25 P.M.

Still pondering, I climb into the front passenger seat. "A ruse." A cover-up. Basically, "I got played."

"Professeur, you not are babbling."

"This is not how I envisioned things to be at this stage of my research and definitely not at this stage of my life. The distractions are overpowering the mission, and other than you and Dublé, I don't know who to trust."

Bilal drives past the Menelik. "Today, I take you to my home."

"Why?"

"Because I should have done so many months ago. I have been working as an interpreter for the past ten years. I have never befriended any of my clients but our experience has made us close. It was always work, work, work then separate. Not so with you. Today I want to take you, my brother, into my world."

I am at a low point and my hope for healthy human relationships is fading so I don't protest. Such a visit might help me to maintain sanity. "I am honored."

Arriving at his home, we remove our shoes and place them by the door before entering. Bilal has managed to maintain a very nice standard of living. He is paid well and is considered a professional man within his family and his community. He is well respected.

I wait in the living room. Anxious.

He calls for Numa and it is obvious that he is more anxious than I.

She gracefully enters the room wearing a beautiful green and red dress with an orange scarf covering her head that highlights her face which resembles a brown porcelain doll. Vibrate brown eyes. A most delicate voice, *"FurSa sa'eeda."*

As a sign of genuine appreciation for allowing me to enter their home I place my right hand over my heart and bow slightly. "I am pleased to meet you too."

With that, she gives Bilal "the look." Culturally, there are some relationship signals that transcend the boundaries of verbal communication. For any man from any part of the world, "the look" from the woman in his life basically means that trouble is brewing and it's headed his way. She smiles and goes into the back room.

"Excuse me Professeur, I shall return." Concerning their conversation, I my not understand their words but I do understand the tone. She is basically doing all the talking and he can't get a word in edge wise. He lets her finish what she has to say. I don't have to know the actual conversation because I have been to enough couples counseling sessions in my day to know that despite the issue, she is right.

Bilal returns and hurriedly walks toward the front door. "Get your shoes we must be going." Remarkably, and for the first time, I see sweat beading across his forehead.

Before I exit, Numa enters the room. Smiles. "Good night, Professeur Dunstin."

Driving to the Menelik Bilal explains that, "Djiboutian City women are not like other women in Africa. They are sometimes aggressive and independent minded. They are outspoken. This goes back to the khat. Many women have had to become the head of households while the men chew the money away. Many are strong of will. That is my Numa."

I did not comment, but I was glad to leave Bilal's home. Numa is young, petite and seemingly very sweet, but I can tell that if he pressed the issue of me staying in their home a minute longer, she would have whoop't his ass and he knows this to be true.

"Is everything okay…with you and your Numa?"

"Professeur, she does not like you. To her you are the man who is going to get her husband hurt again, or even killed. She does not like the way my face is looking with my eye swollen and my bandages. She does not like the fact that we were not able to spend our first night together. She is fearful and it is understandable. Never will I be allowed to forget that I was taken and beaten on the day of our wedding. This will never be forgotten and I will forever be reminded. She does not like you Professeur, and that will not change anytime soon."

"Understood."

He pauses and smiles. "Tomorrow? Early?"

"I will be ready. Tonight, drop me off at the Special Place."

TWENTY-THREE

Monday, June 4, 2007, 9:45 P.M.

Missing Lizette. I recline on a chaise, cigar in the right and Merlot in the left. Lionel Richie understands my feelings, *"Thanks for the time that you've given me. The memories are all in my mind."* I'd never been good at relationships and feelings and all but she brought me a point of satisfaction that made the possibility of commitment worth investigating and now she's gone. It's interesting how the right person can change the dynamics of any situation and in a matter of months Lizette had become that "right person" for me. My *"Three Times a Lady"* and more.

What pisses me off is the lingering notion that she might have been involved in something foul that might have taken her away from me. I want to miss her without reservation but a cloud of doubt is robbing me of the opportunity to think and heal.

I dial. *"Bonsoir* Professeur Dublé. I know it is late, but I was concerned about your well being."

"Thank you Professeur Dunstin. You are truly a credit to your profession. I am doing well under the circumstances. Resting currently. This old man isn't used to being jostled about, but all is well. How is your 'well being?'"

"Uneasy."

"Sherry. My office tomorrow."

"Change it to Merlot and you've got a deal."

"The bumps on the head must have lowered my standards. I will make an exception this time, Merlot it is."

It feels good to laugh. "Tomorrow it is. *Au revoir*."

After talking with Professeur Dublé and finding him in good spirits my mind is somewhat eased. I take a deep breath, "What can I do now?"

I dial. "Ambassador Singleton, this is Professor Dunstin, I apologize for calling so late, but…"

"Don't be silly Dunstin. I always have time for the people. If you're not busy I'll send a car to the Kempinski to pick you up."

"I'll be out front."

"Very well."

I set the half smoked cigar in the ash tray and quickly finish the glass of Merlot. I pick up my backpack and walk to the front of the resort. "How did he know I was at the Kempinski?"

Fifteen minutes later I'm in a black Lincoln Continental limousine heading to the Ambassador's residence.

•••••••••••

The Ambassador's study. Formal greetings abandoned. "How long have you been keeping tabs on me?"

"Since day one."

"Why?"

"Professor Dunstin, you may not realize this but your work has international implications and your success can bring Djibouti to a new level of world-wide attention in a very positive way. I and many others want that to happen. Try one of the cigars in the box on the table. I think we both enjoy the same claro wrapper."

"You know my brand?"

He smiles, "Monte Christo 50's."

I open the humidor on the desk. Three robustos, three torpedoes, and three churchills neatly arranged. Monte Christos, Davidoffs and Cohibas, each with the official *de la Habana* label. Nestled next to these cigar smoker's gems is a damn Swisher Sweet complete with plastic tip. I throw a judgmental glance at the Ambassador as I snip the end of a Monte 50 and light up.

He smiles and shrugs his shoulders, "Something for everyone." He retrieves a Cohiba, snips the end and lights up.

"Being that you've been checking up on me, maybe you can tell me the whereabouts of Lizette? Why couldn't you prevent what happened to Bilal and myself? What about the twins?"

"I want you to understand the big picture about this country and this region…hell, this Continent.   I was appointed to this position soon after 9-11 and at that time it seemed like a useless job in a barren country.   I soon found that I could not be more wrong.

"Djibouti is the smallest of the Horn of Africa countries, and on the surface it seems like the bastard child of the region, but the fact is that everything that is happening in Africa is beginning to pass through here somehow.   Djibouti controls the access to the Red Sea and it is of major importance to the region.   The port has been taken over by the same company that has revamped other ports throughout the world and the potential is huge. In no time, this little country could likely become one of the richest in the world.   The problem is that the port is right now alive with the smuggling of goods, drugs and even people.   The barren lands around Djibouti City make hunger and poverty a reality, but it also makes human exploitation a reality.   The prevalence of khat is no accident.   It has a way of keeping these people in a dormant disposition while others take advantage of their wealth and their resources.   Daily, the local men are lulled into a very high high and a very low low, and during their low is when illegal activities reach their heights.   Port authorities turn the other way when bribed with small amounts of money and bundles of their green Godess.   In Djibouti the rich are profiting while the poor are chewing khat.

"Let me also point out that information following the events on 9-11 have great implications in this region. Islam is the most dominant religion in this Continent and if the extremists find a way to push their understanding of the Qur'an onto the people the impact would be devastating."

"What would prevent that from happening?"

"The reality is that many of the African countries have either recently ended civil conflicts or they are currently engaged in some form of civil unrest. The killings among the tribes and governments in Somalia, Rwanda, Uganda, the Congo, Liberia the list goes on and on. The infighting keeps these powerful countries segmented and that makes a unified radical Islamic uprising improbable. Not impossible. Improbable. Some of these conflicts are publicized but most never receive attention from the international community. The rapes, the murders, and the maiming of women and children are unbelievable and nobody hears about it. So far, it doesn't seem possible to form unified hatred on the rest of the world in the name of religion when you are working harder to kill those that look like one's self."

The Ambassador's insights have explained much. "Thank you for helping me to see the big picture Sir, but what does this have to do with me? I am a scientist, not a politician. I am not involved in anything crooked and by having me followed you should know this."

"Go on."

"What can you tell me about the twins?"

"They appear to be mercenaries. Muscle for hire. They pop up from time to time then go underground. Lately, they've been very visible, as you well know. Why the openness, we don't know, but we are sure that they will lead us to their employers. I have to admit that it is puzzling how they manage to stay one step ahead of our operatives. Satisfied?"

"Yes and no."

"Go on."

"*Yes* because you have some answers, but *no* because you really haven't done a damn thing to make my situation any better. I thank you for the puff and vino but I got a lady to find. Have a good night Ambassador."

He draws deeply the Cohiba, "One more question before you go. Tell me about your dealings with Mademoiselle Lizette Moniette."

"That's something different. That's personal."

"Word to the wise, *it usually starts out that way…*"

I get defensive, "Watch yourself Ambassador. I didn't come here for this kind of…"

"Of what…TRUTH! Sit down Dunstin and hear me completely! *It usually starts out that way* BUT your situation is unique. I don't know how you did it, but you stumbled into something serious. Very serious! The way I see it, you currently have four choices. Go on with your research and stay out of peoples way. Stop your research and play Lone Ranger with Bilal as Tonto and possibly have someone else get hurt in the process. Or you can tuck tail and leave Djibouti only to regret it for the rest of your sorry life." Smoke rings. Impressive.

I sink into the chair, "What's the fourth option?"

"Let me help you."

"Ambassador you have summed up my situation fairly well and I will admit that my options are limited."

"Open your eyes Dunstin. Your best assent is sitting right in front of you."

He's right. I really don't have anyone else to turn to. I feel responsible for Bilal and I want to protect him without getting him more involved. I am laden with guilt over the situation and the whereabouts of Lizette. It hurts and I somehow feel responsible. Hell, I even feel responsible for Professeur Dublé getting roughed up. It hurts. Most painful, I am haunted by the notion that the death of Maxi might have had something to do with me. Damn. I want the pathway of hurt to stop leading back to me and I do want a chance to confront the twins, "So what do you think I ought to do?"

"You can start by telling me the truth about what happened last Saturday night. The bull crap story you served us at the

Chapel just wasn't good enough. Start with the truth and stay with the truth. I need you to be explicit. Recall the sounds and smells. Any words that come to mind. Anything." He then places a voice recorder on the corner of the desk. The red light flashes, "Begin."

I did my best to give the facts while answering any questions that are asked. What do I see around the Menelik. Where do I usually eat? When and where do I wash my clothes. How much time do you spend at the school? How have I been received by those at the Horsed School? Where's the Posse? How much time have you spent on the base? How have I been received at Lac Assal? Whe did I last call home? How much time do you spend with Americans? Continuing on, I finally get around to describing the black Mercedes. What time it was when I called Lizette? What time it was when I went to her flat and found the door kick in? What time did I call Professeur Dublé? What was said in the conversation? When did the van arrive with Bilal inside? How did I feel when I saw Bilal bloodied, bound, with a gun to his head? How long was I unconscious? What did I see? How did it smell? What did I hear? How many were involved? I recalled the events in detail, and by doing so I am even more made to realize just how serious this situation has become. Eyes wide open. The new big picture clarity felt like a kick in the chest and I am gripped with both fear and anger. More anger. I need resolution and I need it soon.

"Okay sir, I've told you all that I know. What do you know about Lizette?"

The Ambassador appears forthright, "Not too much. The Intelligence Report says that she was born in the Cape Verde Islands. She does very well at selling real estate. Her story raises no red flags. The only negative connection she has would be in conducting business with the wrong people and didn't know it. She has worked with all of the notables in the area and that's pretty much it for your lady friend. She's clean as far as we know."

The accusations by Dublé come to mind but I manage to keep it to myself. My second Monte 50 was a pile of ashes when he finishes, "That's good to know but she's still missing. What next? I know it's late so we can get started in the morning right?"

"No."

His response didn't sit well with me, "Ambassador with all due respect, I didn't tell you what happened just so I could be removed from the situation. Of the choices you posed to me over an hour ago the only one that matters to me is that I use your help to find out what is going on!"

"Dunstin! Why do you jump to the wrong conclusions? That is a character trait most undesirable. We've talked right? Hell, we've even smoked. I've given you glasses of my finest Merlot and yet there is no trust between us. Right now it is 12:30 A.M. and I would appreciate it if you would let me damn finish."

"I'm sorry Sir. It's been a rough few days, and I haven't had much sleep."

"No kidding! Now, what I was about to propose to you was the option of not waiting till the morning. We can get started tonight."

"What do you mean? And who is we?"

"Djibouti City is dormant at night. The locals are sleep. Pretty much the only activity conducted at night is either illegal or underground. We can't wait till day break. We need to get started now because I leave for the States in a couple of days. There is a monthly meeting that I attend and it started thirty minutes ago. Tonight you will be my guest."

"Proactive, I love it! Outstanding! So who am I riding with? Brokenbow, or one of the other NCIS agents. State Department Security. Who?"

"Dunstin, you were in the Army correct?" The Ambassador picks up a file marked *CLASSIFIED* that is sitting on his desk. He begins glancing at the contents.

"Yes sir."

"Your service record shows that you served in Lundstuhl, Fort McCoy, Fort Bragg, Fort Jackson and you had a brief hitch in Korea. Your marksmanship scores are excellent, and I see that you were mounted with the 203. You worked in Administration, 42-Alpha, then you were cross-leveled to Postal. Fox 4, Fox 5 with the Top Secret Security Clearance. You were then given the assignment to personally transport classified documents. A dangerous task. Did you ever look to see what the documents contained?"

"No. I was a mule. I did my job. I really didn't care about the contents of the envelopes."

"So you know how to follow orders and you have a sense of the possible consequences when orders are not followed. Correct?"

"Where is this conversation going, Ambassador?"

"When you were stationed at Fort Bragg, did you notice that one of the sender names that constantly appeared on the documents that you couried was Major Singleton."

"Okay."

"You're looking at him."

Big smile, "I knew you looked familiar, but I just couldn't place you! Small world. Major Singleton. Now it's Ambassador Singleton. How bout that."

He elaborates, "Some of the other couriers broke the seals and contaminated the contents. That single act ruined many Army careers, but you were one of those who simply did your job and you did it well. You were very well respected from up the chain."

"Thank you sir. Now, getting back to Djibouti."

"You need to change clothes. What are you about a 44 Long and about 36 or 38 in the waist?" He escorts me to the guest room where the closet boast of a variety of men's suits, shirts, slacks and shoes of various sizes. "You got ten minutes to shit, shower and shave. Everything you need is here."

I didn't question. I cleaned-up, dressed-up, and was ready for business eight minutes later.

I return to find the Ambassador is on the telephone. He says to the person on the other line, "Please hold." He asks me, "What alias do you want to use for the tonight?"

The question appeared odd but my response was immediate, "Dixon."

He continues with his call, "Dixon. D-I-X-O-N. Dixon."

I adjust myself while looking in the mirror. Nice slacks, comfortable and expensive looking shoes and a shirt that resembles the one I saw Tony Montana wear in *Scarface*. The only item that appears unfashionable is the huge gauze bandage that is wrapped around my head. I return to the clothing closet and retrieve a leather baseball cap to hide the uncoolness.

We proceed down the hallway and into the parking garage. The Ambassador is wearing a long sleeve button down, slacks pressed to perfection, shoes immaculate, blue blazer over shoulder.

I will admit that for the first time in along time I feel at ease.

"Dixon, tonight call me Duke."

"Duke?"

"You remember Duke, the leader of the G.I. Joes. Don't tell me you didn't have some Joes hanging around when you were a kid. You should be old enough to remember the gung-fu grip?"

"Had? Sir, I got two in my room right now. They've been traveling with me since I left high school. They guard my belongings. They don't have the gung-fu grip, but I haven't been robbed either."

Exiting the main house the Ambassador mentions, "By the way, your apartment is a mess."

"How the hell do you know about the inside of my apartment!?"

"Heyyy, I'm just sayin'."

"So where are we going? Duke."

"Hear me well. I've got a very important Meeting with very important people. What occurs at the Meeting must remain at the Meeting. Got it?"

"Is this some *James Bond 007* kinda stuff?"

"Just remember. What occurs at the Meeting must remain at the Meeting."

In the parking garage each vehicle is cleaned to show room perfection, except for one. Next to the black Lincoln Continental limousine, the black Mercedes coup, and black Humvee, the two black motorcycles and the two black mopeds, there was an older white four door Toyota Cressida. Clean but old.

We walk towards the Cressida. "You're kidding right?"

"Get in Dixon." The garage door raises and we begin backing out.

"Where's your security detail?"

"Don't need one. Too risky. I trust you."

Now I'm concerned.

TWENTY-FOUR

Tuesday, June 5, 2007, 1:05 A.M.

As I question the Ambassador about what else he knows about me in Djibouti, I notice that we've arrived at the Port de Djibouti. He slowly pulls up to the Main Entrance guard shack. "Duke with Dixon as my guest."

The guard checks his list and speaks into his walkie-talkie. "Pier 17 Sir." He then signals to the other guard, who is armed and wearing a Djiboutian Royal Guard uniform, the gate is raised. We drive the required 10 kph.

I've seen the Port during the daytime, but this can't be the same place. In the light of day there are hard looking people who are also hard working. Commerce. Movement. Exchange. During the day I witnessed the ebb and flow of livestock being sold and transported.

Now, in the darkened alleys and the cluttered stalls the most visible element is the stench. The kind of smell that jumps on every hair of your nostrils and magnifies itself every time you inhale. The mingled smell of the camels in Stable 4, along with the horses in Stable 6, next to the cows in Stable 7, combined with the sheep and goats that are wandering the premises freely. They all come together to form a blend of nasal badness that forces one to surrender without putting up a fight. Add to the essence of the critters, the smell of hay, and the pungent stab of indiscriminate outdoor toilet usage and you have the second worse concoction of atmospheric foulness.

Does this smell rival that of the day before yesterday? No way! That was the smell associated with death. This is the smell associated with life. This smell I can tolerate. That said, neither of us talks because we don't want to risk swallowing huge gulps of awfulness.

The corner lights on the road and in the alleys are dim and the elongated shadows move at a lugubrious pace but it was clearly obvious that the entire dock was alive with the seediest looking characters. Wearied, long faced, Djiboutian and Somali herdsmen and workers lurking in hollow spaces and sleeping, huddled next to their livestock with excrement near. Toothless maritime Irishman, in port for a few days and looking for ways to release some tension. Drunken Englishman, basically looking for a "tussle". French sailors returning to port well passed their curfew. Russian sailors proving the effects of what happens when Vodka is your national substitute for water. Non-descript human life forms are in the corner shooting dice and uttering the universal exclamation, "*Snake eyes!*" All types of people, all types of images. The first word that comes to mind, Zombies.

Knowing the needs and desires of the average guest to the Port, the Djiboutian government does it's best to keep all visiting shipmates and mariners inside the gate. To satisfy their urges there are two restaurants open around the clock. Alchohol is available for the right price. There are prostitutes of all types meandering the alleyways. The mingled smells of cigarettes, cigars, marijuana and apple or cherry hooka fills the air. Add to it, the stringent smells of coffee and fresh human urine and you have the Port de Djibouti around one o'clock in the morning.

•••••••••••

Pier 17. Royal Guardsmen are posted at every corner. We slowly approach the loading entrance of a cargo ship named *CJ Triskett*. The Ambassador gives the names to the guard, "Duke and Dixon."

The guard returns a familiar smile and nods, "Welcome Sir, lights out please." We proceed up and into the open ramp of the ship. I am completely at a loss because Duke has elected not to update me on every action of our journey. The mysterious and covert manner in which we are proceeding is both frustrating and exhilarating. I understand that, "What happens at the Meeting must remain at the Meeting" but that insight doesn't clarify why we are we pulling into an old and rusty cargo ship with our lights off?

Pier 17.

Ascending the darkened incline made the display even more spectacular when we descended into the hull of the ship. Lights. Sounds. A much better caliber of smells. Pier 17.

Once inside the parking area, we are greeted by female parking attendants dressed in frock-tailed coats and fishnet stockings. Like Playboy Bunnies, less the tail and ears. "Welcome to Pier 17 gentlemen. Here are your complimentary gift bags containing a CD of the finest Australian Jazz music, a round of award-winning cheese, two bottles of Australia's best wines, one Cabernet Noir the other Pinot Grigio, and an amazing parfum for the ladies, along with three boxes of Cuba's choicest cigars."

She instructs us to park next to the red Lamborghini Countach. There are three of them. A space is available next to a yellow Porsche Boxster. Duke did the parking while I did the gawking. BMW. Bentley. Harley Davidson. Mercedes. Cadillac. Lincoln. Lexus. Jaguar. Along with the occasional vintage American Muscle Car. Rare and unbridled opulence was on display. I see about forty cars and ten motorcycles, ours the most humble.

We exit the Cressida and walk down toward the pit. I can't keep my eyes off of the twenty-four hand-blown crystal chandeliers hanging from the ceiling. Magnificent.

"Duke, you could have warned me." Pause, "On second thought, I wouldn't have believed you anyway."

We are met by another attractive attendant, "Welcome to Pier 17 gentlemen. May I have your names please?"

"Duke." He signs her list using his assumed name. She hands him a gold plated name badge. DUKE.

"Welcome back sir. And you are…?"

I was half listening while looking around and acting like a true tourist. Rookie.

"Sir, your name?"

"Yeah, ah Carter Dun…"

"Dixon! His name is Dixon!" Duke to the rescue.

She knew the right words to say. "Thank you sir, and being that you obviously are a first time guest I need to give you a few of our house rules. The food is complimentary. The drinks are complimentary. The cigars are complimentary. Our exchange currency for tonight is the American dollar. Opening bid at either of the tables is $1,500. The women are here to help you enjoy and if you desire more from either one of them, I am sure that can be arranged. And do remember that, what occurs in the Meeting must remain in the Meeting. Do you have any questions *Monsieur* Dixon?"

Her delicate voice calling me *"Monsieur"* reminded me of my purpose for being here. Lizette.

"No questions." I sign, Dixon.

"Here is your name plate. Please have it in full view during your stay and please return it before you depart. Dixon, Duke, welcome to Pier 17."

Heading toward the pit, Duke stops, "Take it all in, and then get over it. Your name is Dixon and you deserve to be here. You've earned the right to be here. Think like that, and you'll be like everyone else in the ship. Entitled. Now relax and enjoy."

Another lovely approaches. "Good morning Gentlemen, welcome to Pier 17, can I get you something to drink?"

"I'll have a Scotch on the rocks, he'll have Merlot…chilled and bring me sixty in chips please. We'll be at poker table number three."

I didn't mind him ordering for me because I was too busy being awe-struck. Pier 17. The floor boast of wall-to-wall burgundy carpet that rest on a frame anchored by massive hydraulic stabilizers, keeping it completely level despite the movement of the participants inside and the pulsing waters outside.

Level. The entire setup is an engineering masterpiece and an architectural work of art.

The walls are finished with brick and stucco, holding an impressive collection of some of the most expensive original paintings. Picasso, Warhol, Van Gogh, Rembrandt, Renoir, Dali and Lawrence to name a few. The apparent theme of the works of art seems to be garishness. Pure and unbridled. Garish.

An L-shaped bar in the back provides an area for fine dining. Four culinary masters appear to be cooking everything to order and made to perfection. I hear the Australian jazz band that is positioned in the rear to maximize sound and to enhance the fine dining experience. The silent but powerful central air cooling system is helping to provide an atmosphere of comfort without zapping the air of the splendid mixture of food, smoke, drink, and conversation. "Gentleman place your wagers." It's all for one's pleasure. Pier 17.

Three blackjack tables, three roulette tables, three poker tables, seven old school "one arm bandit" slot machines, three billiard tables and magicians doing card tricks up close. "Tricks are for sale" boasts one card master. "Everything has a price."

There is a currency exchange section with a vault bigger than a Humvee and I'm glad the exchange for tonight is the dollar because I'm not too good with that Djiboutian franc stuff.

It feels like the finest of Las Vegas and Monte Carlo rolled into one all in the hull of a cargo ship. The lights flashing. The sounds. The beautiful women. Men of all nationalities with one thing in common, money and lots of it. Pier 17.

"Dixon, its time to conduct business." We walk over to table number three where the game is Texas Hold 'Em. Duke asks, "This seat taken?"

"Yours," responds a portly man that resembles the Prime Minister of Djibouti…it is the Prime Minister of Djibouti. Having been taken by the décor and the engineering brilliance of the vessel I have paid little attention to those around me. I slowly scan the faces of the men in the room only to find that I am currently in the company of some of the most powerful men in the world. African elites, Arabian sheiks, European businessman, Asian company owners and American high rollers all gathered on an Australian cargo vessel, the CJ Triskett, in the Port de Djibouti at Pier 17.

I can't believe what I am seeing, but as Duke instructed me, I act as if I belong. Entitled.

The Prime Minister's real name is Diya al Din Hasani, but his nametag reads "Raphael". Also at the table are other notable participants, each sporting their chosen moniker. The Indonesian businessman, Harvey; the Belgian sports team owner and restaurateur, Justin; the Kuwaiti oil magnate, Memphis; and the South African businessman, Dean.

The Dealer announces, "New game gentleman." Cards dispensed. The young lady arrives with the Scotch on the Rocks, a chilled Merlot and $60,000 in chips. She receives a hundred dollar tip.

Duke pulls me close and whispers. "Tonight, you are my guest. Enjoy." He hands me $10,000 in chips.

Speechless.

He returns to the game, "I'm in." The Dealer deals.

There are armed guards all around the vessel. Some are Djiboutian Royal Guardsman which only service the President and the Prime Minister. Standing among them are an international blend of armed military personnel, private security, and a variety of policemen.

I leave Duke at the poker table and walk over to the Blackjack tables where I scan the international list of notables.

Djiboutian President Mukhtar Sugal, aka Boris.

Arabian Sultan Ahkmed Bashir, aka Lester.

Retired NBA Hall of Famer, Felder Hampkins, aka Luke.

Qatari business developer, Arnon Jelawi, aka Quenton.

Russian utilities owner, Vaceli Berishnikof, aka Harlan.

German physicist, Leonard Ziepling, aka Festis.

Admiral Chester from Camp LeMonier, aka Euclid.

My goodness, Chaplain McCreary, aka Sebastian.

That almost looks like Fidel Cas…naw, couldn't be.

I don't know the stories or the titles that go with the others in the room, but it is clear that every man is here because of his position, wealth, alliances or name. Arrogance. Bravado. Pier 17.

The Camp LeMonier contingency is wearing civies, but I am surprised at how many military uniforms are represented from other countries.

I walk over to the bar. "Scampi over linguini cooked in olive oil and topped with a healthy dose of parmesan please."

"Very good sir."

I find a seat that affords me the best view of the festivities. Shortly thereafter, I feel someone breathing on my earlobe accompanied by the words, "I knew I'd run into you sooner or later."

I turn. "Sahar from the dance club. How are you?" Warm embrace. My food arrives. " Are you hungry? Would you care to join me?"

"I'll pass.but I'd be honored."

Her beauty has not escaped, she stills possesses the spark of someone who has not lost her will to fight. The twinkle in her eye. I ask, "How long have you been coming here?"

"This is my third time. A friend asked me to work here and it was the best one night I've had. I've been invited back every month since."

"So this happens once a month?"

"Yes, and it's always on the first Tuesday of the month. It starts with the ringing of the bell at one minute after midnight. You don't appear to know much about this, who did you come with?"

"Duke." I point to him at the poker table.

"Oh Duke, yes, nice tipper. Great shoes. What did he tell you about Pier 17?"

"Nothing really except, 'What happens at the Meeting stays at the Meeting.' What more can you tell me about this floating playland?"

"The rest of the world is not aware that the greatest collection of the most powerful and influential men on the planet meet in Djibouti, Africa once a month at Pier 17. The only thing that changes is the host country."

"What do you mean?"

"Today the host is Australia, last month it was Greenland, and the first time I came it was Brazil. That's why we are in an Australian cargo vessel. Australian items in the gift bags. An Australian jazz band. All of this is to say to the guest, and to the rest of the wealthy world, that Australia is a great host. Let's do business."

"So the other times you attended, there were other cargo ships, or is this the only one?"

"Each country had its own. The Brazilian cargo ship was fitted with two levels complete with gaming excitement and two sanctioned boxing matches. Along with other things."

"I won't ask."

"Good, cause I won't tell." We laugh. She gently strokes my hand.

While eating, I watch as Sahar carefully surveys room, taking in her surroundings. "I can only imagine the business deals, the buildings being built, the military agreements being made over games of chance. In this one place."

Complements to the chef. "Speaking of games of chance. Blackjack. Let's give it a shot."

We find a table where no one is sitting. Dealer's challenge. "Place your bet!" I put $1,500 on the table. Two cards dealt. 9 of Clubs and 6 of Hearts.

"Hit." Card dealt. 5 of Hearts. Hold.at 20.

The dealer shows a 10 of Hearts. He flips his down card. 8 of Clubs. He pulls another card. 5 of Diamonds. Busted.

Sahar jumps with excitement and hugs my neck as the dealer declares, "Winner!" Chips are passed my way.

"Shhh, keep it low, I don't want to attract attention."

"Dixon, I get paid to be the one who draws attention to you. Get used to it." She kisses me on the cheek and whispers, "Thank you for coming here tonight."

It wasn't long before our table became the hot spot. Onlookers and participants. Win a few, lose a few. I quit while I'm well ahead. The flow of the game works best when you do what works, and stick with it. Monotonous maybe, but if it works why change? Must be the researcher in me.

We move to another table, joining a threesome. Blackjack that is. I lose the first hand because I hit when I should have held. On the second hand I get back into my rhythm. I quickly adapt to the different Dealer. I get in sync with his pulling the cards from the Shoe. The different cadence. The different seat. Sahar is now on my left shoulder. Feels rights. "Go for it!" I place my entire $19,500 on the table. People gather. The dealer pulls from the Shoe. I get a 10 of Spades and a 4 of Hearts. I looked to see what others have.

Trudeau is in the first position, he has a 2 of Spades and a Jack of Spades.

Montague, has a 10 of Hearts and a 7 of Spades.

Billy, a 6 of Diamonds and a 3 of Clubs.

Trudeau taps and receives a Queen of Hearts. Busted.

Montague taps and receives a 7 of Clubs. Busted.

Billy taps and receives a 2 of Diamonds. He taps again, 5 of Clubs.

"Hit." The dealer sends me a 5 of Hearts. I hold at 19.

My 19 to Billy's 16. He taps. Queen of Diamonds. Busted.

The dealer has an 8 of Hearts. He reveals his downcard. 8 of Clubs. He pulls one more card. 9 of Diamonds. Busted.

"Winner!" An abundance of chips are pushed in my direction. Sahar screams with excitement. Applause erupts from those around the table. I collect my winnings. Throw a thousand to the dealer. I'm done.

"Dixon I am so happy for you!" Big hug.

"You're my lady luck." I kiss her on the check. Nice warm embrace. "My hands are full, let's go take care of this." We both carry the chips to the Bankers table. "Chip exchange. Larger amounts please. A thousand broken down."

Arm in arm we walk to the slots. Old school one-armed-bandits types. "I never forgot you Dixon."

I think to myself, "Oh boy, here we go."

"The first time we met you showed me how nice it would be to just cuddle, laugh and talk. I wasn't ready and I've regretted walking out on your invitation. I never forgot you. The way you looked into my eyes. The way you actually listened to me when we talked. Your gentle massage on my back…my legs. I wasn't ready then, but if you ever have time, I'd like to try again."

Is it because I'm temporarily rich or is she sincere? This is the same chick that went ghetto Jekyll and Hyde on me a few months ago. "The offer is tempting and tonight you are truly my Lady Luck, but I'm actually looking for a very dear friend. She was kidnapped three days ago. Her name is Lizette Moniette?"

"Her name doesn't sound familiar, but pretty women are often kidnapped and sold into slavery and have to sell themselves to buy back their freedom." Her words declare her plight.

"I know Sahar and I am very sorry. What do you know about a pair of angry African twins that drive a black Mercedes with a smiley face." Her expression changes and her body tenses. Her beautiful brown face becomes flush and tenses with a look of fear and anger. More anger.

She asked, "Do they have your friend?"

"They do."

"If you ever see her again, she will never be the same."

Pushing for information, "What do you know about them?"

"They are devils. They are twin devils."

I remove the leather baseball cap to display my bandages.

She nods in disbelief. "Are you sure you want to pursue this?"

"Continue."

"Their names are Boulos and Butrus Aideed. They boast of being in wars in Rwanda and the Congo. True or not, I don't know but I am sure that they are Somali."

"How do you know?"

"Their language betrays them. Believe me, they are Somali. They have been involved with the conflicts in Somalia were they served as rebels fighter and led massacres on innocent people and villages. They are nomadic thugs. *Kilaab*. Animals. They roam the area and they take and trade things that do not belong to them. They are exporters of the worst kind. Trading women, children, drugs or anything that can give them profit. Their hearts are black. No feeling. No concern. Cold and black. They can hear the cries of a young woman pleading to be released and their answer is to beat her and rape her until she is quieted and her fight is seemingly gone. They laugh like hyenas. Curse the day their mother gave them birth. Worse, curse their mother! The merchants and even the pimps no longer deal with them because the goods they deliver are usually damaged and unprofitable."

I gently hold her by the hand, "I can tell this is not easy for you to talk about, but I really appreciate your help. I really need to know who they trade with and where can I find them?"

"I hear they operate out of a storage warehouse somewhere near the here. They trade with whoever has the money, or whoever wants to buy what they have. They are opportunists. Their spirits are damned and their hearts are black. They are animals, just animals. *Kilaab*! They take advantage of people and have no allegiance to anyone but themselves."

●●●●●●●●●●●●

"Duke, don't you think we ought to meet and finish the proposals before you *get away.*"

"You have my word Raphael, there will be time for that."

"You seem uneasy. What troubles you?"

"Raphael, what do you know about a real estate agent named Lizette Moniette?"

"She sold me some land to build a house for my daughter near the sports stadium. I got a very good price. Why do you ask? Check."

"She's missing."

"That's unfortunate. She is quite a beautiful girl who knows her business. She is very well respected. I will get started on that situation in the morning."

Memphis chimes into the conversation, "I know Lizette Moniette. She can't be missing, because I conducted business with her last Saturday morning. As a matter of fact she met me at the tailor shop near the French shopping district. She was there to close a land deal, but I was there to try on a new custom blazer, silk inlay of course with the 18 carat buttons and before I could finish my transaction Mademoiselle Moniette, with the help of the tailor's apprentice, had pulled an absolutely hideous powder blue with black polka dots dress off the rack. The dress was from the

House of Perineesee in New York and it was absolutely hideous I say. Well, she went to the dressing area, put on the dress, and reappeared looking tailored in every dimension. Stunning. On her the distasteful blue with black dots came alive. 'Perfect size 4,' the tailor remarked. She turned to display her new find, to which I could only say, 'Allow me to make this purchase for you.' I not only bought the one for her, but I ordered eight others ranging from sizes 2 to 18 for each one of my wives. The total cost was $18,000. We signed the contract at the clothiers and the last I saw of Mademoiselle Moniette she was sashaying down the strip in that beautiful new dress. Fold." Cards thrown in.

"She went missing that same day. The door was kicked at her apartment and she's disappeared. It looks like kidnapping."

"Like I said Duke, I'll have my sources ask around and see what information can be found in the morning. Not here. Game." Raphael wins the hand.

"You lucky bastard. We'll talk later today." Duke collects his remaining chips and gets up from the table. Lights a cigar and starts for the bar.

A tall man with curly blonde hair, sporting a traditional black tuxedo, sidles up to him. He extends his hand with a hearty Aussie greeting, "G'day mate. My name is Wilhelm, your host for tonight's Meeting." Actually, his attire betrayed him, the host is the only one at the Meeting allowed to wear the classic black tux.

"The accommodations are exceptional. My name is Duke."

Wilhelm lowers his voice and leans in, "I overheard your conversation and I think I might have encountered the young lady you inquired about."

"Continue."

"We arrived into port three days ago. On Sunday me and my business partner Ulysses, were introduced to several of the local politicians and businessmen."

"Yes, the welcoming party. I normally would have joined them but I had some pressing matters. Go on."

"On our way back to the pier our vehicle was flagged down by a two Africans. Ulysses and I were well armed so we stopped. No fear. They got out and came to our vehicle. The two Africans were twins and they were driving a dark green van. One came to the driver's side and one to the passenger side. On cue, Ulysses and I got out of the car. Our weapons were displayed but not drawn. The two men stopped and raised their hands. They showed no weapons and they kept smiling as if to be friendly and at this point we didn't suspect anything. No fear y'know?

"No fear. I got that. Continue."

"The one driving began talking and saying, 'We know that you are businessmen. You are shippers and traders. We want to trade with you.' I asked what they had of value. They motioned for us to come to the side of the van. Broad daylight. They seemed to pose no threat. One talked while the other opened the sliding door. The van was filled with stuff, cheap imitation cigars, and gaudy jewelry, but sitting on a blanket was a beautiful woman, hands tied, mouth gagged, feet bound. She appeared to be weary as she tried to motion for our help.

"Ulysses doesn't say much but his large physique can be quite an intimidating asset so he took over the conversation. We both noticed the girl. We looked at one another, and he said, 'How much for the lot, Mate?'"

"'Two thousand American.'"

"'That include the girl?'"

"They begin to laugh, 'What girl?'"

"Not knowing what was worth the giggle, and not being clear on what was happening, we start laughing too until Ulysses says, 'That girl.'

"They stopped with the laughing and the one pulls down his sun shades and looks at us through bloody red eyes and slowly says, 'There is no girl.'

"To which Ulysses slowly replied, 'There is no deal.' We stepped back to our vehicle, hands on our weapons, and before we get in the local police pulls up beside us and asked, 'Problem?'

"One of the twins reaches inside the van. Grabs a bundle of that khat they have here and hands it to the *Blue Heeler*. 'No problem here.' The police drive off and we got in our car and returned to the ship."

"The police were no help. Did you try anyone else?"

"Duke, this is Djibouti mate, a bundle of khat buys silence even from the *soggies*. Who else could we tell? Besides, this is Africa, who cares?"

"How do you know that was the same woman I was asking about?"

"She was wearing the powder blue dress with the black polka dots that Memphis described."

"Where did they stop you?"

"We were leaving the Government Buildings, it was by a parking lot and, oh yes, it was by the roundabout not far from the huge statue of the Djiboutian warrior."

"Thank you. Here's my card. If anything else comes to mind, call me directly or you can reach me at the Embassy." Shaking hands, "Great job with the Meeting."

•••••••••••

Sahar and I are playing slots when I see Duke waving for me. I walk over, and Sahar follows carrying the winnings. "Damn Dixon, how much have you won?"

I smile, "Last count over fifty grand."

"Good, then you can give me back the ten I spotted you, with interest. I'm long on information but short on chips." Sahar stands close. "Who's your friend?"

"Sahar meet Duke. Duke meet Sahar. She and I go way back…she knows."

"She know the rules of the Meeting?"

"She schooled me."

"Good enough. We don't have much time."

"What do you mean?"

"Lizette Moinette was seen the day she disappeared…"

"Duke, I talked to her that day. I know this already."

"Dixon, this cutting me off thing is really starting to piss me off."

I back down, "Rough day. No sleep."

"No kidding!"

"Continue."

"Thank you. She was seen the day see disappeared while conducting business, but someone also saw her later that day in the back of a green van, tied up and gagged. To top it off, the drivers were your African twins."

"Where can we find them?"

"Hell if I know?"

The Final Bell sounds. One hour till daybreak. This bell alerts the men to finish their games, settle their accounts and get home and get cleaned up for the next day's work. It also alerts the Muslims that *al-fajr*, the dawn prayer, is approaching.

"Let's get going, Duke."

"Dixon, I've got to make a deposit and you have to take care of your winnings."

Sahar and I walk over to the currency exchange tables. There are several transactions taking place but a sufficient amount of Bankers are there to conduct business in an error free and expeditious manner.

Duke places his chips on the table. The Banker then takes a scanner and touches it to his golden nameplate. "Deposit $36,500 no cash out." He completes the transaction. No receipts are given. The account balance will float to the next Meeting. Cash can be provided upon request.

It became clear to me that a computer chip is embedded in the nameplate and it has all of the pertinent information of that particular participant. DIXON. The phone call Duke was making while in his office made this possible. The ten grand was my starter amount, he had already transferred it to my account, or should I say to the account of Dixon. We place all of my winnings on the table. The Banker confirms, "Your total Monsieur is $52,650.

Thinking quickly, "Put $23,500 in Duke's account. Give me $3,000 in cash. The remainder goes to the girl."

"Monsieur, all of our support staff are very well paid, such a contribution is not expected."

I have a headache and I am tired. I am in no mood to be told how to spend this money. I speak slowly and at a whisper, "Monsieur Banker, credit Duke's account $23,500 now!" He does. "Give me $3,000 cash now!" He does. "How much is left?"

"$26,150 remains."

"Give my lady friend $20,000 cash. Whatever is left you keep."

"But Monsieur…" as the Banker begins to protest, Duke discreetly catches the eye of Ulysses, the other host in the black tuxedo, who is observing the interaction. Ulysses discreetly nods to the Banker to accept the offer. The Banker hands Sahar, $20,000 cash. The Banker then pockets $6,150.

"Thank you, Monsieur. Please, do come again."

Sahar stands there not believing what has transpired.

Duke is ready to go and could care less.

She and I embrace. I kiss her on the cheek. "Thank you. You are very special. I hope this is enough."

"Enough for what?"

"To buy your freedom."

"This is enough to get me killed. You can't just leave me here with this. Take me with you."

I wasn't thinking clearly. "Duke, she's right."

"Hell no Dixon, we've got enough to deal with already and we don't have much time."

"Sahar, he's right this isn't the time for…"

"I can help. Take me with you, besides if I try to leave with this money I may be the next girl to disappear. I'm scared. Please, take me with you. I can help."

"Dammit Dixon, let's go!"

Our dealings with the Banker were witnessed by others. A businessman named Manfred who is sporting the garb of a sheik was not to be outdone, he loudly declares to his Banker, "Take $10,000 for yourself!" Pointing to three of the lovelies in black, "You! You! You! Come and accept this $10,000 as a token of my appreciation."

Before long, others were following suit and attempting to out-tip those that were around them. The entire scene was garish and childish, but what would you expect with a ship filled with the most influential men on the planet. Testosterone and opulence, a lethal cocktail.

Duke finds the perfect two words to explain this reaction, "Dumb asses."

We return our nametags to the Greeter. She is the friend of Sahar who invited her to the Meeting. Sahar discreetly hands her $1,000. Cash. *"Shukran."*

Her friend is dumbfounded, but most appreciative, "*Afwan. As-salaamu alaikum.*"

"*Wa 'alaikum as-salaam.*" They embrace.

We reach the parking area. We walk past the exotics. We avoid the Euro-models. Past the Muscle cars. Straight to the Cressida. I hold the back door open for Sahar to get in.

She looks at the car and remarks, "You're kidding right?"

"Suit yourself." Duke gets in and starts the engine.

"Okay well, let me get my bag!" She goes over to the closet where the ladies personals are kept and retrieves her large blue bag. She puts her $19,000 inside and runs back to the car. "Okay so you're not kidding." She climbs in the back.

TWENTY-FIVE

Tuesday, June 5, 2007, 5:25 A.M.

A line of vehicles, ours and the ornate, caravan out of the hull of the *CJ Triskett* and away from Pier 17. The stark contrast between the "well to do" to the "well done" was harsh and seemingly unfair. I just witnessed a floating wonderland of the most lavish display of materialism and greed only to find that those who need the most are forever going unnoticed by those who have the most. We exit with windows rolled up and air conditioners blowing. We are elite and the privileged, I doubt if any in our convoy noticed the decay of the human condition inside or outside of the Port. Proceeding through sadly lit roads, we say very little.

When exiting the security gate of the Port de Djibouti, the vehicles in the caravan peel in various directions. The sun is beginning to peak and the glow of a new day is dawning.

I look back to notice that Sahar has reached into her bag, and changed into a blue sweat shirt and sweatpants. She's had practice. She leans forward and removes the leather baseball cap from my head. She lightly touches my bandage and gently rubs the back of my neck. "The twins?"

"Yes."

"Do you want revenge, or do you just want to find your lady friend?"

The question had merit and required momentary thought before answering. *Do I want revenge for what they did to Bilal, Dublé and myself? Do I want revenge for what they might have done to Lizette? Or would I be content to simply find Lizette and be done with it?* The question had merit and I could sense that the Ambassador also wanted to know the answer. *How far was I willing, or wanting to go?* "Well I…stop the car! STOP THE CAR!"

We pull to the side of the road. Screeching halt! "Dunstin, what the hell!?"

"Look!" To our left we see a black Mercedes, darkened windows, with a yellow smiley face on the passenger side of the rear window. Parked in front of it is a dark green van. Both vehicles are next to a warehouse about two blocks away from the entrance to the Port de Djibouti.

The lights are on inside so the Ambassador pulls into a vacant lot about 100 yards away, on the other side of the street. He parks and turns off the vehicle.

Eager. I begin to improvise. "I'll be right back!"

"Dunstin, stop! I didn't bring you with me just to be pushed aside when its time to do some heavy lifting."

"Ambassador, I appreciate it, but this is where your importance overrides the mission…" Before I could finish the Ambassador had exited the vehicle, removed his sport coat and was running toward the building, motioning for me to check the front window.

I did so and he went to check the back area.

We met on the side by the vehicles.

Whispering, "What did you see around back?"

"A regular metal door next to a garage-type door. There's also a window with bars on it. What'd you see?"

"The twins are in there. One is sitting in a chair to the right. The other is standing next to the wall with a clipboard. I did see a rifle in the corner to the left. I say we go through the front door." We nod in agreement.

"Wait!" The Ambassador produces a Gerber, which is a multiple use tool. He exposes the blade. "This is all I got. Grab something solid." We then canvas the immediate area for items to use in our assault.

I pick up a pipe. "Hand me the Gerber?" I use it to puncture the sidewall of the four tires on the black Mercedes.

The Ambassador returns with a thick cable about two feet in length with a large bolt secured to the end. Handing him the Gerber, "We have to go in now, it's almost full sunrise. The call to prayer will be issued soon."

"Cool it Professor. Let's go in after morning prayer, it'll give us a few more moments to prepare." We agree to wait. The call for *al-fajr* is announced by the muezzin from the mosque's minaret and about a minute later the front door begins to open. They are coming out.

"NOW! NOW! NOW!"

With the rhythmic sound of *Salah* in the background, the Ambassador and I force them back inside the door. The element of surprise was on our side, and not being prepared for the attack, they both fall backward. Butrus' face bounced off the door when we entered, opening a gash on his left temple. Dazed, his .357 Magnum drops. The Ambassador jumps to retrieve it and they begin fighting for the weapon.

I swing the pipe in my hand and hit Boulos in the back of the head with the anger of a man who had been dropped off in a valley of dry bones. I heard the *thud* as he hits the ground, face first. I kneel down and begin checking his pockets for weapons. Nothing. I pick up the .357 Magnum. "Stop!"

Butrus stops fighting with the Ambassdor and raises his hands while his back is turned toward me.

Blood has splattered on the Ambassador who handles the rare dishevelment rather calmly.

Butrus demands, "What do you want!? Are you come to steal!?"

"Turn around." He does so, slowly. Through the blood that is flowing from the open gash he recognizes who I am and starts laughing. His laughter seems cloaked in decadence and defiance. I want to shoot him.

He laughs. *Does he not fear the impending outcome? Does he not have any regrets? I am holding the gun! He laughs! I'm pissed!*

The Ambassador checks him for weapons. "Dunstin, lower the weapon, he still has value."

The Ambassador was not trying to appeal to my moral center. He was tapping into my military psyche which was always trained to decide if a target had value or not. Lizette was still missing. He had value.

He stops laughing, "It was just business, Professeur."

"Business with who? Why?"

"I cannot tell you, but you will never see the girl if you hurt me or my brother."

The Ambassador finds a spool of packing twine and scissors and uses them to tie the hands of Butrus behind his back.

He does the same to Boulos who is unconscious on the floor, now lying in an expanding red pool of blood.

Butrus notes, "My brother needs care."

"You have got to be kidding me. You bust my head wide open and leave me among death and disease and now you think I give a damn if your brother has a little scratch on his head."

The Ambassador uprights the chair that was knocked over during the scuffle. He directs Butrus, "Sit down!"

Boulos, not fully conscious, but fully covered in blood is then set up and leaning against a pallet of grain.

Butrus sees the Gerber, with blade exposed, is on the floor by the bags of flour and when *Salah* ends he stands and protest, "You did not give me time for prayer!"

The Ambassador pushes him in the chair, "Shut up and sit down!"

"*No al-fajr*! *No al-fajr*!" He then falls to his knees and onto his side next to the bags of flour. "*Salah*!" He has the Gerber.

"Prayer time is over. Wait till midday! Now get up and sit down!" The Ambassador picks him up and places him back in the chair.

"I want answers. You have attacked me, Bilal and the Professeur named Dublé? I want to know why, but more importantly, where is the girl?"

He only laughs and says nothing. Unknown to us, he is actually working to free himself.

Our interrogation stalled, "Ambassador, why don't I go get Bilal and he can help us to get some answers."

"Goodness sake man, I can't be left here alone."

"Good point. Well, why don't we just leave Sahar here with them."

"No that would be too risky. How far away does Bilal live?"

Perturbed, "You should know where he lives, you been following us around since I got here!"

Asserting his authority, "You need to check yourself, Professor!"

"You're right sir, I'm sorry. I haven't been sleeping lately."

"No kidding!"

"I got it! Why don't we take them with us, get Bilal, and then we can interrogate them where ever we damn well please." I felt like a genius.

"That's why you're the Professor, but I got a better idea…"

At that moment, Butrus rushes towards me and knocks the gun out of my hand. Before the Ambassador could react, Butrus picks up the firearm and is motioning for the Ambassador to stand next to me. "Hands up!"

Gun trained our way, he moves toward his brother and gently shakes him. *"Akh. Akh!"* He begins to vigorously shake him, but there is no response. Boulos is breathing but is not conscious. *"A'taqid an al-iSaaba jaseema!"*

Butrus waves us over to the far corner next to a pallet of rice. He picks up his brother and sets him in the chair. Butrus then leans the chair back on the rear legs and begins dragging his brother across the floor to the front door. He then raises the gun to shoot, "I am not instructed to kill you but I will make an exception."

WHOOSH!

Without warning and with force, the door swings open! Our eyes adjust as the room fills with sunlight.

It's Sahar and she's holding a .38 handgun! She commands, *"Yaqif!"*

Butrus, back turned to the door, raises the hand holding the gun over his head. The Ambassador secures the weapon.

Butrus leans the chair forward on all fours. He raises both hands and turns to see who has entered and taken control of the situation. He sees the eyes of Sahar and commences to laugh and begins to move toward her.

With finger on the trigger, she softly utters, *"Kilaab."* Trigger squeezed. *BANG!* For the span of maybe a millisecond, she is eye to eye with her tormentor and takes pleasure in seeing the look of disbelief on his bloodied face as the bullet enters his forehead and exits through the back of his skull leaving splatter upon the dry goods.

Butrus falls limp into the lap of Boulos who, at the sound of the shot, regained consciousness only to witness the body of his lifeless brother falling upon him and to the floor. Boulos begins calling, "*Akh! Akh!*"

Sahar puts the gun to the head of the remaining twin. He begins to sob.

With finger on the trigger, she softly utters, "*Kilaab.*"

Having seen what happened moments before, I shout, "Sahar stop! Don't shoot! We need information from him!"

Determined to exact her revenge, "He does not deserve to live."

"I know, I know. You can kill him later. I promise." I was trying to appeal to her well focused anger.

"You promise."

The Ambassador is standing there holding the gun. I look to him to play along, but he shrugs his shoulders, "Hey, she's your friend. No offense Ma'am." Again, I look to the Ambassador to help me out, "Yeah whatever, you can kill him later."

She lowers the gun. Boulos continues sobbing.

"Sahar why didn't tell us you had a gun?"

"You never asked."

The Ambassador and I confer. "She is right." "Yeah."

I begin questioning Boulos who sees his mirror image bloodied, disfigured and laying on the floor. Eyes half open.

"Why did you attack me. What were you looking for?"

He sobs, "*Akh! Akh! Akh!*"

Sahar presses, "Let me do the same to him, so I can shut his damn mouth." She places the gun to his head. "*Yatakal-lam.*"

"Not yet." I gently help her to lower her gun. To him, "You will soon be like your brother if you don't start talking."

He sobs. Sniffles. "We were given instructions to beat you and Bilal, but we were instructed not to kill either one of you."

"What about the girl? Where is she?"

He murmurs and begins to black out. The blood streaming.

"He's got a concussion." The Ambassador begins shaking him, "What are you saying?"

Boulos motions toward the left of the room. "There."

I see pallets. "What are you saying? Where?"

The Ambassador and Sahar keep watch over Boulos. I pick up the pipe and walk behind the stacked items.

I find a storage room. I remove the opened lock that is securing the latch. I open the door.

"Lizette!"

TWENTY-SIX

Tuesday, June 5, 2007, 7:01 A.M.

Lizette stumbles out of the storage room. We embrace.

"Are you alright?"

"Oui."

Having prepared for the worst, what I saw was not expected. She seems exhausted and little else. She does not appear to have been harmed, wounded, or worse. To the extent that her clothing became her tracking device she was clean and wearing fresh clothing.

"Are you all right? Did they hurt you?"

She held my face in her hands, "Oui Monsieur." We kiss and embrace. "You don't look so good though."

Blood on my shirt. Bandage on my head. "I haven't been sleeping much lately."

Over the items on the palettes I hear the Ambassador, "No kidding!"

She tenses, "Someone else is here?"

"Friends. They helped me to find you. Have you been here all of this time?"

"Oui."

I briefly look around and inspect the storage unit where she has been housed. It is more of an efficiency apartment. Other than the thick, sound insolating walls, the amenities are rather pleasant. Air conditioning, carpet, chair, television (with cable), DVD's, bed with clean linen, kitchenette, stocked refrigerator, shower, sink, toilet, it was all there. Creature comforts.

I ask again, "You've been here all of this time?"

"Oui."

"You *were* kidnapped correct?" I regret my skepicism.

"Oui! It was awful. I heard footsteps outside my door and thinking it was you I opened it and in rushed three men wearing black clothing and black mask."

"Three men?"

"Oui."

"You let them in?"

"Unknowingly, yes!"

I call to the Ambassador, "Are you hearing this?"

"Every word."

"Lizette, we need to leave, but I want to warn you that things on the other side of these palettes is not very pretty."

"Let me get my things." She turns and goes into the room and comes out with an overnight bag, her purse and her keys.

"They let you keep all of this stuff?"

"Oui, but they took my phone."

We round the stacked items only to reveal the carnage of this damnable situation. Lizette is startled by what she sees and recoils into my arms. The massive display of blood, the dead man on the floor with back of his head opened, the lingering hint of gunpowder, the bloodied man bound and sitting in the chair, Ambassador Singleton standing there with a gun in his hand, and Sahar waiting for Boulos to make a false move so that she can put a bullet in his head. It was a sight.

"Lizette, this is Sahar and Ambassador Singleton."

"Pleasure." "Hey."

I continue, "When I got to your flat the door had been kicked in. Your place had been trashed. There was evidence of a struggle."

She protested, "I would not know. After they came into my home, two of them restrained me in the chair while the other one put a towel over my face. I can remember was the sweet smell that was on the towel. When I awakened, I was in the storage room.

Seeking clarity, "So, all that happened Saturday after I left you that morning."

"Yes, later in the day. Earlier I met with a client."

The Ambassador interrupts, "At a clothing store with a Kuwaiti oil man who brought you a powder blue dress with black polka-dots."

In unison, "How did you know?"

He smiles, "I know a guy."

Without investing further thought into his comment she continues, "They put a bag over my head and took me to that storage room. They woke me up the next morning, and gave me some fruit. After eating, I was bound at the feet and at the hands and I was gagged again with a bag put over my head. This time they put me in the back of a van and removed the bag. They drove around trying to conduct business as if I didn't exist. By the end of the day I was exhausted and hungry. Then they put a bag over my head again and brought me back here. They untied me and I walked in to find that my overnight bag was inside the room lying on the bed. It had toiletries and clean undergarments and other necessities like a gown to sleep in and this pants suit with socks and tennis shoes."

Gesturing toward Boulos and Butrus, "Do you recognize these men?"

"Oui Monsieur. They drove me around in the back of the van. They were trying to sell some salt crystal sculptures."

The Ambassador asks, "What the heck are salt crystal sculptures?"

I answer, "You know, the animal skulls that are dipped in Lac Assal. It forms a thick covering of salt around them. They sell them in the market."

He nods, "Got it. Carry on."

She continues, "There were three meetings. At each stop they took two salt sculptures with them, and when they returned to the van minutes later they were pocketing a lot of money. While in the van they would make a phone call, simply to say that the deal was done."

"This is good dear, continue talking. What else comes to mind?"

"Another thing I noticed, each meeting was conducted during *Salah*."

I ask, "You mean during prayer time?"

"Oui, the first was during the dawn prayer, the second during the midday and the last was during the late-afternoon. I didn't see who they were meeting with in first two meetings, but the third exchange took place on the street. They pulled the van over to the side of the road and waited for about ten minutes. I heard the muezzin announce the call to *al-'asr*. I was very tired so I faked as if to be sleep. They got out and met with, at least, two men."

I asked, "How do you know who they met with, if you were tied up in the back?"

The Ambassador throws his hands up, "Dunstin, there you go with that cuttin' people off crap! Would you let her tell her own story? Please excuse him, Mademoiselle. Continue."

"Merci. I know they met with two men because the four of them came to the side of the van, opened the door and conducted business in my presence. Though I faked sleep, I parted my eyes enough to see them. It seemed odd that neither of them seemed concerned or alarmed that there was a woman in the back of the van."

The Ambassador interrupts, "Describe to other men?"

"They were either Australian or New Zealanders."

He continues, "Was one a tall thin man with curly blonde hair?"

"Oui! Oui Monsieur! And the other was a broad and muscular man. They looked at the sculptures and paid $40,000 for one and $70,000 for the other. At first, I thought they said Djiboutian francs, but they were dealing with American dollars."

The Ambassador is miffed, "One hundred and ten thousand dollars! What exactly did they buy that could add up to that much money?"

She reiterated, "They purchased two ram head salt crystal sculptures."

I raised my hand to be recognized, "Lizette, allow me a moment for clarification, are we talking about the ram heads that are dipped in Lac Assal and over about a month's time the salinity of the lake collects on the dipped object and when it is pulled from the water it is covered with almost a half an inch of pure white salt?"

Ambassador, "This is not a scientific expedition. Get to the point!"

"Are we talking about the same salt crystal sculptures?"

"Oui! Just as you describe."

"One hundred and ten thousand dollars for two souvenirs that are worth no more than twenty dollars a piece at the town market!" The Ambassador begins pacing.

"The first time I ran into these guys was Thursday of last week. Bilal and I were at Lac Assal. They were buying something from the merchant, whose name is Na'im, it could have been those salt crystal sculptures. I wasn't paying them much attention." I begin pacing.

While the Ambassador and I are basically walking in circles and trying to find answers, Sahar brings clarity to the situation, "Gentleman, the guy who sold the stuff is right here. Why don't you just ask him?" She and Lizette share a girl-power high five.

"Well, I guess we could."

I lean close, "You were selling something more than salt crystal sculptures? What was it?"

"I cannot tell."

"Who were you working with, besides your brother?"

"I cannot tell." He begins to laugh. Like his fallen brother, he has a laugh that should only be reserved for pack animals.

"Tell me," I hold out my hand and receive the gun from the Ambassador. I point it at the head of Boulos, "Tell me, or I will make you like your brother." I heard that one on *Kojac* some years ago.

"I cannot tell."

The Ambassador bends over and pulls up his pant leg, retrieving a cell phone from an ankle holster that was made to hold a .22 handgun. He presses one button. "Brokenbow, I need you and three of your best interrogators to come to the 112 Warehouse on Avenue General Galleni. Bring the Roadie. No sirens!"

"Aren't you going to call and have the *CJ Triskett* apprehended?"

With regret the Ambassador looks at me and responds, "Dunstin, what *CJ Triskett*? Never happened. There is no manifest for that ship, in that port, on that night. It was never there and you and I were never there. Worse, would be to attempt to apprehend the ship and then have to face the international response by those in attendance. It wouldn't be good either way. For all practical purposes the *CJ Triskett* does not exist."

I continue, "It would have been nice if that holster had a .22 instead of a phone."

"Dunstin, think again, a .22 has six bullets. The right call on this phone at the right time will bring 6,000 bullets within minutes. The way I see it, the same holster serves the purpose of carrying a lot more fire power."

"Why didn't you use the phone when we were outside?"

"I didn't know what we were up against. Sometimes, things are not as they seem."

Something the Ambassador just said kicked my mind into high gear. The salt crystal sculptures are worth twenty, yet they were sold for thousands. "That's it! Thank you Ambassador! Things are not as they seem."

I lean in toward Boulos, "What were you transporting in those skulls!" I retrieve my phone and begin dialing.

"You really don't know what you are asking?"

"Bilal, I need you to get to the 112 Warehouse on Avenue General Galleni. Now!"

Boulos continues laughing. "Silly, trusting and naïve."

"Who?" I demand. "Who!"

Boulos continues, "We are traders and that is what we do. We trade different things to the highest bidder. We trade with others who trade."

I persist, "Who is *we*?"

He remarks, "I say no more."

"Think about it Ambassador. Khat is daily. No need. Marijuana is not an issue. There are other drugs in Africa. Accessible. Easy to get. Think about it Ambassador. The Pier 17 Meeting was a front for…"

•••••••••••

WHOOSH!

Again the front door swings open while nine Royal Guardsmen immediately fill the room. Guns are drawn and trained on each of us. The light from the early African sun impedes our vision in this dimly lit warehouse.

"*Gaacmaha kor utaag!*" Startled, we each put our hands up.

"*Hubka dhig! Hubka dhig!*"

Sahar and myself slowly put the handguns on the ground and back away.

"*Joogso!*" Neither of us moves while we are searched.

The Guard giving the orders goes to the door and announces, "*WaaDiH!*"

With that, Prime Minister Diya al Din Hasani fills the doorway, lighting his cigar. His cadence is slow and deliberate, "This is a messy situation Ambassador. Have we lost trust?"

The Ambassador stands his ground, "I must ask you the same, Mister Prime Minister. Why are you here?"

"Based on the fact that there is a dead African on the floor I need not answer. However, I value our working relationship so I'll share with you that after our most recent conversation at a table I was concerned about the young lady's whereabouts. I attempted to reach you at the United States Embassy this morning but you had not returned. A search had confirmed that your vehicle was in this area. Add the fact that we have had this warehouse under surveillance by the Municipal police for possible illegal activities my presence is well understood. So, I ask you again Ambassador, are we experiencing a breach of trust?"

Agent Brokenbow is allowed to enter the room, while the other NCIS Agents wait outside. Seventeen in all.

The Ambassador responds, "No, Mister Prime Minister there is no breach of trust between us. The young lady I was looking for has been found. Unharmed. Her captors are here. One bound and one dead. My people are unharmed."

"Very good Ambassador Singleton. It appears to me that the Djiboutian Royal Guard will have to explain to the Municipal police about our interfering in a joint operation and apprehending the suspects in question. Just so you know, your lady's captors are very dangerous men. They have been accused of money laundering and dealing in illegal trade. They are also accused of Crimes Against Humanity in Somalia."

Boulos begins to laugh.

The Prime Minister is stern and unflinching, "Did I say something to amuse you?"

"I make money trading and you know it. Illegal or no, who cares. This is Africa. In Somalia we did what we were ordered to do." Boulos then spits on the floor in front of the Prime Minister.

SMACK! Boulos is rapped on the cheek by the Guard in charge. "*IHtiraam!*"

The Prime Minister offers a cigar and the Ambassador accepts, "Ambassador Singleton, you and your party were not here. In the future should you find yourself in any position of compromise while in Djibouti you are welcome and strongly advised, to call me before it gets to this point. We will clean this up." The Ambassador bites the end of his cigar and the Prime Minister sets it ablaze.

Our guns are returned to us. The Ambassador reaches to shake the hand of the Prime Minister and notices the blood, he then nods and exits. The Prime Minister then turns his back on Lizette, Sahar and myself as if to compound the suggestion that we were never there.

The differing perceptions about the twins are made obvious as we depart. Butrus dead and Boulos is bound and bloodied.

Sadly, they seem to represent all that is disturbing and vile about humankind. These so called traders have existed only for the purpose of satisfying material and political gains. Though the twins might have benefited, they have been played as pawns in other men's games. Boulos and Butrus were not operating alone. They did the dirty work for someone whose hands, at least for now, are clean.

Filing past Boulos, Sahar, with gun in hand, leans towards him and mutters, "I should have killed you while I had the chance. *Kilaab*!" She spits in his face.

Lizette appears grateful and relieved. She sympathetically smiles at him and walks out.

I have no opinion concerning the twins. I know that they were merely following orders. I do, however, have to reconcile with the enjoyment they expressed while carrying out their heartless orders. They took pleasure in inflicting the pain of blunt trauma to another man's skull. They were overjoyed when they threw us, bound, from a moving vehicle into the field of the dead. They probably reveled in beating up on the defenseless Henrì Dublé. They so savagely assaulted my Lil' Buddy that people have grown cold and silent. It appears that they've delighted in raping and murdering and stealing. I cannot comprehend such a soul-less mindset. They take pleasure in the pain of others, and I have yet to understand their purpose. Here too, I have not been told who was behind this operation or why.

I reach down to pick up Lizette's bag filled with her personals. I meet eye to eye with Boulos whose head is leaning to the side. I ask, "Who were you working with?"

"You don't want to know." He then mutters, "I regret killing the boy."

"Me too." My immediate instinct is to inflict pain or punishment to accompany his admission of guilt but I maintain my rage, "Who ordered this. Give me a name!"

He manages a bloodied smile, "Good fortune on your insect find."

Humanity momentarily restored, "*Shukran. As-salaamu alaikum.*"

"*Wa 'alaikum as-salaam.*"

TWENTY-SEVEN

Tuesday, June 5, 2007, 8:18 A.M.

Bilal arrives as we begin loading into the vehicles. His look of surprise and hesitation could not be masked. Members of the Djiboutian Royal Guard are armed and standing at the ready. NCIS Agents are loading into unmarked and common vehicles, except for Agent Brokenbow and three others who load into a vehicle that is larger than a conversion van, but smaller than a bus. Haggard and weary, the four of us lean against the Cressida and allow the events to marinate.

Bilal approaches, *"Subax wanaagsan."*

"Good Morning, Bilal."

"Professeur, either you've had a very late night or a very early morning?"

"Both my friend. Both." We smile. Manhug. "Everybody this is Bilal." The response is an anemic, "Hey." I continue, "Bilal meet Sahar and Lizette, you already know the Ambassador."

"I am honored. So Professeur, what is on today's agenda?"

"We ride to Lac Assal."

"When?" Everyone appears caught off guard by my response.

Without hesitation, "Now."

The Ambassador questions, "Are you sure this is necessary Dunstin?"

"Yes Ambassador. Very necessary. By the way Sir, I have a favor to ask of you. Is it possible for Sahar and Lizette to stay at the Embassy until we get back?"

"Request granted, just keep in mind that tomorrow I am leaving for Washington, but we'll talk more about that later. Right now, I need a shower."

Bilal and I start toward the Mitsu, "I'll see you all later."

The Ambassador remarks as if standing behind a podium, "No, you won't. It's been a very long night. Serious events have taken place and the implications are yet to be understood. Two ladies have earned their freedom. Two brothers have been separated between the dead and the living dead. At this very moment, it's hard to tell the good from the bad. Now is the perfect time to cleanse one's body, relax one's mind, plan the next move and go forward."

I interrupt, "Yeah but…"

The Ambassador throws up his hands. "Dammit Dunstin, there you go with that interruption crap again. I give a good speech after a hard fought victory and what do you say, 'Yeah but.' I even thought I heard stinkin' violins playing in the background. Birds were singing in unison. Had I not been interrupted, one of you would have felt a tear dancing over your cheek and what do you say, 'Yeah but…' Hey, how bout next time I just say that you ain't goin' no where, cause I gotta go home and take a shower and you ain't leaving without me. Get in the car!"

I ask, "So you're driving with us?"

"No, you and Bilal need to follow us to the Embassy. You're riding with us in that." The Ambassador then points to the vehicle of choice…the Roadie.

•••••••••••

We arrive the Embassy shortly after nine o'clock and Sahar and Bilal are reluctant to enter. She, from Ethiopia having functioned as a sex merchant. He, a Djiboutian, a local. Both were looking for the rear entrance. It is the same in Djibouti as it is, or has been, in many other countries where locals are not permitted to enter certain buildings, public or private. This same reality of separatism motivated the Jim Crow laws in the American

South, the caste systems still in place in many areas of Indo-Asia and the recently abolished apartheid in South Africa.

The Ambassador pulls Agent Brokenbow aside, "I need you to give these ladies the speech about keeping the events to themselves and not to share them with my wife. Then escort Bilal and the ladies inside and introduce them to Emmie."

As they enter the door together, I follow the Ambassador as we duck in through the dining room and then to the guest room. He instructs me to, "Get cleaned up and change clothes. I can't let her see us like this." He then leaves for the Master Suite.

"Ambassador…HOOAH."

"HOOAH. Get dressed!"

●●●●●●●●●●●●

Emmie comes to the kitchen and is introduced to Sahar, Lizette and Bilal. She greets each one with a warm embrace. "Thank you Agent Brokenbow, now you and Bilal can wait in the sitting room. Sahar and Lizette come with me."

She leads them upstairs. "These are your rooms. The clothes in the closets are for you to change into. Find something your size and wear what you'd like. If you need anything just find me or ask someone on staff for help. The Ambassador called and

196

told me that each of you has had a long night, so I'll leave you both to rest, but I expect you downstairs for dinner at six this evening."

●●●●●●●●●●●●

Lizette thanked Emmie and closed the door to her room. Her journey from the Cape Verde Islands to being educated in England, having lived in France and having visited several other countries have exposed her to the experiences that have molded her "cultured" world view. The atmosphere and the accommodations at the Embassy were very much appreciated, not as much for the décor, she has seen better, but because of the warm hospitality and the feeling of safety. Lizette removes her clothing then showers to remove the unpleasantness of the last few days. She looks through the closet to find a "nightie" in her size. Climbs into bed. "Thank you, God." Sleep.

●●●●●●●●●●●●

With genuine appreciation, Sahar thanked Emmie again and again. Tears tried to well up in her eyes, but the five years of learning to hide her emotions forced them into retaliation. She closes the door behind her. Silence. Loud and uncharacteristic, silence. Soothing and healing, silence. The audible ability for the ear and the mind to rest has not been appreciated in her experience. Stolen as a young girl, raped and sold into sexual slavery, she's never experienced such settings of peace and security except in someone else's world. Standing there, with the silence cleansing her soul, she is empowered by the notion that her change has come.

She walks over to the bed. Standing there, she accepts the notion that it's beckoning warmth and relaxation was for her to enjoy, and not for the enjoyment of another. Setting her bag on the floor, she takes three steps back, then runs toward the bed. Jumps! Perfect swan dive.

Lying there, she receives the sun through the window with a renewed sense of vision and wonder. Hopeful. She rolls over on her back and stares at the ceiling while taking in this newness. Breathing deeply. Freedom.

She gets out of bed, picks up her big blue bag and heads for the shower. She removes her shoes, the sweat suit, the fishnets stockings and underwear along the way. She then empties her bag on the countertop. Out comes the tail-less and ear-less black bunny outfit, make-up, a change of underwear, the $19,000 cash and her .38 handgun. She picks up the weapon and holds it. She sniffs the barrel still tainted with the smell of gunpowder. She sees herself in the mirror, looking first at the weapon. Then, at her hand holding the weapon. Then, at her naked body. Placing the gun on top of the money she then turns the water on and enters the shower.

Her time under the falling droplets of water was lengthy and luxuriating, scrubbing constantly as if to wash away the dirt of the last five years. Emerging from the shower, she goes to the mirror and wipes away enough condensed steam to see her face. She brushes her teeth. Combs her wet and beautiful black hair. She puts lotion on her skin. She makes no attempt to make herself look good for others to appreciate. No powder, no eye shadow, no eyelash enhancer, no red lipstick, nothing. Standing there, the steam in the room and on the mirror subsides and she sees herself. Eye to eye. For the first time, and on her terms, she actually sees that she, Sahar Lamis Ayele of Giyon, Ethiopia has grown to become an attractive and intelligent woman.

She gathers the money and gun and then lays naked across the bed...alone. Not having to share it with four other young women in her same position. Not having to wait for someone to arrive in the room to violate, to fondle, nor to dehumanize her. No longer waiting for someone to direct her to do the unthinkable. No more pimps promising protection while inflicting pain. No one attempting to usurp her dignity and control her will. For the first time in a very long time, she rests...alone.

With money in hand, she goes over and picks out a gown made for her relaxation and comfort. She then sits on the edge of the bed. Silence. Soothing and healing, silence. She counts the new currency, bundled in 1000's. *"One hundred, two hundred, three hundred..."* *"Twelve thousand seven hundred, twelve thousand eight hundred..."* *"Eighteen thousand eight hundred, eighteen thousand nine hundred, nineteen thousand dollars. Nineteen thousand dollar!"* She wants to scream with excitement but she has learned the harsh lesson that, "It ain't over till it's over." Stacking the money, she is saturated by a feeling of empowerment and opportunity. Long overdue. Freedom in her grasp. Silence, her soothing new friend.. She places the money under her pillow. She then lay her head on the softness of the same and closes her eyes. Sadly, the ultimate price was paid and a life was taken for her to achieve such serenity, but because of that ultimate price a life was gained. The thought of killing another human never entered her mind concerning Butrus and Boulos. In her mind they were never considered human.

Kilaab.

Dogs.

TWENTY-EIGHT

Tuesday, June 5, 2007, 12:06 P.M.

The Roadie is black, much like a small-bodied Winnebago. Taking a closer look it has the capabilities of a very nimble tank that also possesses an enormous amount of firepower. It's outer shell is sleek but up-armored to withstand rounds from handguns and mortars. Bullet proof windows. It's interior is a beautiful combination of comfort and high-tech gadgetry complete with blinking lights, tracking devises, navigational systems, stealth technology and an intricate weapons panel controlling the turret mounted retracting .50 caliber, the side mounted M14 repeaters, .203 launchers over the front and rear fenders and a front end laser with the capability to slice through ½ inch metal in twenty seconds. Each weapon fully retractable giving the Roadie the appearance of a nice touring vehicle. Nah, forget that, the Roadie, with its smoke windows and adjustable hydraulics now set the city low profile is one tough looking ride.

The two middle Captain's chairs are occupied by the Ambassador and myself. Bilal is up front, doing the passenger glide for a change. Agent Brokenbow is driving and the other members of his team are Agents Derrick Redd, Frankie Smalls and Wanda Holden. Agent Brokenbow never offered his first name, but I figure with a cool name like Brokenbow why mess it up.

"Dunstin, I think she's worth the trouble."

"Who?"

"Lizette."

"Thank you Ambassador."

"Emmie also gives her the thumbs up, so you are welcome to have your wedding at the Embassy."

"Whoa! Who said anything about getting married?"

"Dunstin, I've lived long enough to know that you don't get too many chances like this one, especially when it's right." He continues, "Bilal, you married?"

He turns his chair around, "Yes Sir."

"How long?"

"This is day four."

"Congratulations. Stay that way. I hope you don't mind me saying but it is good to see that you don't have that black crap on your teeth. Keep it up."

"Thank you Sir."

I interrupt, "Ambassador, I got two questions. The first one

Is, why is this called the 'Roadie'? The second, why do you seem so wired up?"

Brokenbow, "Let me help you with the first question Sir. This vehicle is technically called a Multi-Terrain High Tech Rover. Being a veteran you know we love our acronyms but in this case that would be M-T-H-T-R. *'Mother'*. We called it the *Mother* for a little while but the comments got old, *'That's a bad ass mother.'*

Ambassador. "The lamest most predicable comment was, *'That black van is a bad mother...Shut yo mouth.'* It's been the Roadie ever since."

"Well, kudos to the team who took a mini-van, stretched it out, added an arsenal and basically pimped the hell out of it!"

"Not a team. One man   I'll introduce you to the designer. Retired Air Force. One of the best." The Ambassador picks up his thermos. "To your second question. Have you every heard the story of coffee?"

"No Sir."

He then asks, "Bilal, you know the legend of coffee don't you?"

"Yes Sir."

"Would you please educate the good Professor?"

"According to legend, coffee, called *qahwa*, was invented in Africa. An Ethiopian farmer was taking his goats out to graze. It was during the dry season so he went out further to find greener plants. His goats were seen eating from a peculiar plant with buds. Shortly after, he observed the goats jumping and kicking about. Only the goats that ate the buds from the bush kicked and jumped. 'Ah ha,' the farmer thought. He collected a basket of the buds, removed the beans and boiled them. And that is how we came to have coffee."

The Ambassador nods with approval, "Thank you Bilal. Dunstin, in this thermos is some of the same Ethiopian coffee. It is not for the weak of heart or stomach. A few sips of this, and you'll be jumping and kicking too."

"Well Sir, I'm trying to cut back on jumping and kicking so I'll pass this time. I think I'll just take a nap."

"Suit yourself Dunstin. I've got work to do before leaving for the States tomorrow, and if I don't do it now, it won't get done. Agent Holden is the satellite activated?"

"Yes sir."

I close my eyes and try to avoid the paranoia of not knowing who to trust. I also try to avoid the sinking feeling that I finally find the right woman and she's a damn khat dealer. Gee whiz.

Eyes resting, I hear Brokenbow ask, "Are there any special instructions before we get out of the City?"

"No." The directions to Lac Assal from Djibouti City are rather simple. Go West past the Balbala District using road N1.

Continue on N1 then turn right onto N9, which will take you Northwest to, and past, Lac Ghoubet. Take a left onto N10, you are then descending into Lac Assal. When riding past Ghoubet, Bilal and I always turn the air conditioner off and roll the windows down to acclimate ourselves to the furnace-like effect of riding downward into one of the lowest places on the earth.

Interestingly, in all of our time of working together we have never stopped at Lac Ghoubet. Going to Lac Assal you can't miss it. It's there to the right when going, and to the left when leaving, but neither of us has shared any desire to stop. Ghoubet is a very deep lagoon with a single small inlet from the Gulf de Tadjoura. The water is deep and has an eerie turquoise blue color. Beautiful and somewhat hypnotic. Legend has it that creatures often emerge from the lake and kill unsuspecting visitors and in the language of the locals Lac Ghoubet is translated, "pit of demons."

When I started mapping my research I decided that if nothing is found at Lac Assal by the end of month seven, then I would take my researching efforts to Lac Ghoubet. For that reason I don't acknowledge Lac Ghoubet because it represents failure at Lac Assal. To date, my optimism and arrogance won't allow me to contemplate the notion of failure. It is simply not an option. Bilal has said that he doesn't acknowledge Lac Ghoubet because the townies of Djibouti City know better than to trifle with the lore of the locals living around the lakes.

Wiping the slobber from the side of my mouth, I am alerted by the lack of movement. Agent Holden is at the console using the satellite to map the area. The others have exited the vehicle. "What's up? Where is everyone?"

"We stopped." Genius observation, as I collect myself.

"Where is everyone?"

"Outside checking the perimeter and hooking up the winch."

"Winch?"

"Yeah, there's an abandoned car in the road. Question, are there usually abandoned trucks and cars in his area?"

"Yes, a few. Some Dutch developers were trying to collect and transport salt a few years ago but they only succeeded in leaving behind large dump trucks and bull dozers. They're rusted out and just sitting. Why?"

"By the images from the satellite I see vehicles in the area. Most are moving as normal but a few are showing no movement at all but the infrared indicator shows warm engines."

I exit the Roadie. "Ambassador, what's the situation?"

"Somebody left a car, with four flat tires, completely blocking the road is the situation. Now help me hook up this winch up so we can get moving." Having secured the cable around the rear axle of the debilitated ol' Dodge, Brokenbow returns to the Roadie. Agents Redd and Smalls are armed with M16A3s and are patrolling the area. Bilal is assisting with the vehicle removal. The winch retracts and the car is moved to the side of the road. We quickly reload and continue our journey.

Smalls breaks the uneasy silence, "That was no accident, Sir. What are the chances that a car completely blocks the road with four flat tires? Was that vehicle there before Professor?"

"First time. I think we need to keep our eyes open."

The Ambassador, "I agree. Something doesn't feel right. Any other vehicles in the area Agent Holden?"

"Yes Sir, they appear to be abandoned, but the Professor has vouched for their existence."

Brokenbow checks with Holden, "Are we clear to proceed?"

"Affirmative."

Getting excited, the Ambassador comments, "Hell, I kinda want to see what somebody is trying to keep us from, let's get going." He then retrieves the cell phone from his ankle. "Mister Prime Minister, are you aware of any reason why the road to Lac Assal would be intentionally blocked? We are on N10 about to descend. Can you send someone to meet us? I don't know what to expect, but we're ready to proceed."

Due to the screaming voice coming from the reciever, the Ambassador holds the phone from his ear. The Prime Minister has ordered us to turn around and return to the city.

Still holding the phone away from his mouth, "*I can't* (pause) *you* (pause) *Prime Minister* (pause) *it* (pause) *meet* (pause) *at the* (click)." The Ambassador actually hangs up. In disbelief we each cast judgmental glances in his direction. He shrugs, "What!? Bad connection. *'Can you hear me now?'*" Laughter. "Proceed."

We are on high-alert for something and what it is we are not sure. The remaining road to Lac Assal is passable. We continue without difficulty.

When we arrive, Redd and Smalls exit the vehicle. Weapons readied. One left front. One right rear. They check and secure the perimeter. Redd gives the all-clear. Again, with the exception of Holden we exit.

Bilal calls out for Na'im who, for the second time, has not responded to the sound of a vehicle.

The Ambassador requests, "Take me to your work sites?"

Brokenbow cautions, "This may not be a good idea sir."

"I'll be the judge of that. Proceed Professor."

"I would be honored Sir." We walk across the salt and sand encrusted ground that with every step announces our presence to Site I. I explain that there are three sites established in differing geological areas of these mountains. The carcass in the wire cage was a plunked chicken and research is being done to determine what is eating it and is it common, or known. Blah. Blah. Blah.

Little remains of what I call my work, having not been here over the last few days my specimen are dried and seemingly unusable to the untrained eye, but I see possibilities even now. I explain, "My normal routine involves about six hours of on-site research every few days. Cataloging pictures, examining samples, on-site testing, you name it. All in the name of science."

"You mean to tell me you spend six hours out here. This hot and naked land and you've been doing this for the last seven months? In this sun? Unprotected? Looking for something that you don't even know exists?"

I smile, "Yes Sir, that's it exactly."

"Dammit Dunstin, I like your tenacity. Insect or not, I'm gonna make sure you get noticed for your efforts. You can be sure I'm gonna tell the President about you, your work, and what's the name of that school again?"

"Clarkmore, Sir. Clarkmore University in Atlanta."

"That's the one! He will hear about the fine work you're doing. A great American researcher!"

"Thank you Sir. Now, here is where I…"

Brokenbow interrupts, "Sir, a bird is coming in. We need to return to the Roadie immediately."

They turn and run toward the vehicle.

This place has been my focus since I arrived, my entire life and my professional reputation has been invested in this place and at these Sites. I was honored to share my work to the Ambassador but in my heart I know that as these current events are unfolding, my return here seems less likely. I take, what might be my last mental picture, then turn and leave. No time to check the other Sites. I see the helicopter.

Returning to base, I see Bilal talking with Na'im. Their conversation seems animated and argumentative. Hand gestures appear assaultive. I watch as Na'im pushes Bilal in the chest. Bilal swings and misses. Redd pulls them apart.

I run toward them, "Bilal, what is going on here?"

"Professeur, he is accusing me of causing all of this commotion."

The helicopter descends and gently lands. The blades stop and the door opens. Two Royal Guardsman exit and check the area. All clear. Prime Minister Diya al Din Hasani slowly steps down, smoking his trademark stogie.

"Ambassador, I never knew that my magnetic personality would cause us to meet so soon." He offers a cigar. The Ambassador accepts.

Biting the end, and gesturing for a light, "Mister Prime Minister, I am sorry that our telephone connection was not satisfactory. I was not requesting your presence; I was merely trying to inform you of the complete blockage of one of your secondary roads."

"Thank you for your concern Ambassador but I believe that is…how do you say…*bullshit*."

Bilal and Na'im resume their arguing. They begin throwing punches and Redd again separates them.

The Prime Minister turns toward the two, and begins walking in their direction, *"Magacaa? Magacaa?"* Knowing Bilal, he asked Na'im for his name.

Na'im repiles, *"Maxaad radtaa."* Meaning, "What do you what?"

The Prime Minister replies, *"Iaq raali ahaw?"*

●●●●●●●●●●●●

POP!

The distinctive sound of a single gunshot echoes from across the lake!

Everyone takes cover as the Guardsmen, joined by Redd and Smalls, return fire in the direction of the distinctive sound of the shot. Lack of target identification didn't stop an impressive and immediate response. Empty shell casings hitting the salt encrusted floor. The smell of gunpowder floating through the air. The sound of crisp, echoing shots fill the air. Silence.

During return fire, the Prime Minister has returned into the helicopter. Holden immediately pulls the Roadie forward to collect the Ambassador, Brokenbow and myself. Redd and Smalls are with Bilal and Na'im.

I can see the devastating response through the front but I shaken only when I hear Redd reporting over the radio, "Man down. We have a casualty. Civilian."

Fear grips. "Bilal."

POP!

POP!

Two more shots fired!

Our response was even more awe-inspiring. Along with our automatic weapons used to answer the meager attack, I saw the tail of a small rocket leave the helicopter and hit top of the ridge on the opposite side. Impressive destruction! Soon after that, another missile leaves the helicopter hitting the ridge in a different area to the right. Oh yeah!

After about two minutes of no return fire and complete silence, a Guardsman speaking English shouts from the helicopter, "Ground units are on the other side! One is dead! Another is alive, but has been apprehended!" Two minutes later, "The area is secure!"

Redd radios, "One of the civilians is down. I repeat one of the civilians is down. Bring the medical kit."

Smalls gives the "All clear," for our side of the lake.

I jump out of the Roadie and run to my friend, my brother. I go to where Bilal and Na'im were arguing and I am relieved to see Bilal standing. Getting closer I see the fallen Na'im. Shot in the chest. Dead. The flow of crimson slowly making its way into the cracks of the white crystallized floor.

I escort the crestfallen Bilal to the Roadie. Inside are the Ambassador, Brokenbow, Holden, the Prime Minister, and a member of the Royal Guard. Holden leaves the steering wheel and returns to the console and announces, "By satellite, there appears to be normal vehicular movement in the area."

"Thank you." Brokenbow then begins an impromptu interrogation of Bilal, "What were you two fighting about?"

Bilal lifts his head, "He wanted me to stop bringing the Professeur. He said it was bad for his business."

Brokenbow repeats the question, "Why were you fighting?"

"He said that he would send people to hurt me and my wife if I did not stop bringing the Professeur. He knew my wife by name."

I interrupted, "Did he have something to do with our being beaten and kidnapped?"

Bilal responds, "Yes Professeur, he did! He also said that he would not allow distractions to his business."

"Excuse for interrupting but what business!" I ask. "The man sells handmade souvenirs!"

Bilal lifts his head again and speaks softly, "Professeur, we have underestimated Na'im."

The Ambassador chimes in, "Bilal, what are you talking about!?"

"*Maas.*"

The Prime Minister reacts, "*Maas*! Are you sure!"

The Ambassador bellows, "Would somebody tell me what the hell *maas* is!?"

Bilal and the Prime Minister respond in unison, "DIAMONDS!"

•••••••••••

The death Na'im is a serious matter and the Djiboutian government is expeditiously handling all arrangements. For years, visitors to Lac Assal were serviced by this slight man with large hands and feet. I overheard the Prime Minister say that a vehicle has been dispatched to his home to provide the family with proper notification and transport. Scores of Royal Guardsman are arriving in trucks and are being dispatched around the area to conduct a complete search..

I watch as Bilal and a Muslim Guardsmen respectfully and ceremoniously cleanse the body with water, offer prayers, then wrap the body in white linen. At the same time I hear the Prime

Minister report that the dead body of one of the apparent assailants is being taken to the morgue at the Royal Guard Complex for examination and the wounded accomplice is being sent to the infirmary for treatment and will then be held in the detention area and made available for immediate questioning. Both were shot in the back.

The Ambassador retrieves the holstered cell, "Sweetie, I don't think we'll be home for dinner."

There were three abandoned semi-truck trailers in the area. I had often seen Na'im and his sons retreating to them and my guess was that they considered them home so I never ventured to be so rude as to go near the worn structures which were rusting away like the vehicles that were left behind. Though I wondered, I never asked about their living space and the questioning by the Agents revealed that Bilal had never gone into their private domain either but a canvassing of the area revealed many hidden truths about the poor Afar trader named Na'im and his sons.

I walked with the Ambassador to the semi-truck trailors and was amazed to find them more like a lairs. The buildings were fitted with electricity that was provided by generators that were placed in holes dug underground and covered over with sheets of scrap metal. Inside were laptops, tracking devices, mattresses, and in the corner piled high, the water that we been bringing. There was a schematic panel that noted the location of remote motion sensors in the area. One had been placed at the entrance of road N10. Its seems that these sensors gave advanced warnings of approaching vehicles or people walking along the network of trails. It also seems likely that this was how they were alerted to cut the power to the generators as they would humbly appear over the ridge, ready to help the trinket buying visitors. We estimate that they accommodated between three to seven vehicles per day and their sales amounted to very little yet the high-tech contents of the trailers tell a different story.

The Ambassador and I were summoned by the Prime Minister to inspect the contents of one of the trailers. Inside was parked a well-maintained silver Toyota Four-Runner. On the rear window, passanger side, a yellow smiley face sticker.

Information found in narrative journals, financial ledgers and on the computer in the trailers quickly revealed that the simple and destitute trader named Na'im was anything but simple and destitute. Putting the evidence into perspective, he was connected to a pipeline that funneled diamonds and other black market goods into the open market.

The diamonds he funneled are "Dirty" diamonds also referred to as "Blood" or "Conflict" diamonds. They originate in African countries that are ripe with inner conflict. In these countries there are rebel forces that basically do not adhere to local, national or international laws and selling these illegal diamonds helps to fund their activities. They are generally produced through the slave labor of men, women and children. It is also known that these rebels, traders or other opportunist will rob the mines of legitimate miners and sell their goods on the open market. The human tragedy is amazing and the monetary gain is astounding.

Na'im's operation appears to have been simple but very effective. He would receive the diamonds directly through people like Boulos and Butrus. A few others apparently would bring the conflict gems directly to him. He would then pack the diamonds in bags of salt, complete with tracking devices, and have them delivered to specific locations. For centuries, the Afar nomads, would trade salt as a highly prized commodity all the way into the lush and green Ethiopian highlands. Lac Assal is one of the starting points of the nomadic trade routes that, when networked effectively, allowed Na'im to transport almost anything from one place to another with precision. The nomads have used these roads for commerce, whereas Na'im used these trade routes, and his own tribesman, for his own greed and gain. The nomadic traders were never told what was packed in with the bags of salt but are learning that handsome bonuses would be paid to those who delivered the bags to specific locations. The money earned by a nomad paled in comparison to the money that Na'im was making on the black market. Records in the trailer revealed he was the regional leader while were peons and if curiosity set in concerning the contents of the bags supposedly filled with salt they would never return home.

Accessing his computer helped us to piece the information together. We were also able to map his network and we found that several vendors in the City did business, not with Na'im, but with the twins. A phone call from the Prime Minister to those securing Boulos confirmed the finding that in a variety of ways raw uncut diamonds were transported into and out of the Port de Djibouti and they were also circulated through select buyers in the Market Square.

Though veiled, the transport of the gems occurred in open view. Dirty diamonds were hidden in bags of salt accompanied by a tracking devices. The most prized diamonds were cut to release their brilliance and were secured in a small burlap bag and attached to the inside of the skull of a ram, a bull or an antelope which was then submerged into Lac Assal for a month thus creating the highly valued salt crystal sculptures.

Na'im and his sons had cornered the manufacturing market of the salt sculptures and also the distribution market. According to his records, which date back several years, Na'im was very well paid for his services and collaborating with opportunistic thugs like Boulos and Butrus only helped his operation. Warehouse 112.

One journal, with several narrative entries over the years, detailed how Na'im had formed alliances with partners who, like himself, were getting older and the delicate balance of tradition and respect was teetering with the intrusion of younger, more aggressive traders. Noting how the operation was turning against itself, he began making changes to secure himself and his family. In, what appears to be his latest entry, he sent his two wives, six of his sons and his two daughters to Addis Ababa, Ethiopia. The two sons that I was familiar with, Nadir and Yasir, had been sent to stay with family in France.

Four Royal Guardsmen had returned from the home of Na'im. They were sent to notify the family. I overheard as they detailed the upscaled modesty of the home of Na'im in the outskirts of Arta. I listened as it was reported how the home was fitted with the latest amenities and exceptional creature comforts. The Guardsmen reported traveling about two kilometers and questioned his nearest neighbors. They reported that Na'im had mastered the art of living well without display. He never appeared in public except to go to work at 7 A.M., much earlier than anyone else and he returned home late in the day. Those that could make the connection were afraid to do so. Tribesman maintained secrecy and honor and locals rarely go to Lac Assal, for fear of having to pass Lac Ghoubet. The pit of demons.

Though the mystery of Na'im was unfolding, several issues remained unsettled. Na'im didn't originate the diamond trade. He was a major player but served as a conduit to disperse the goods.

Whom did he collaborate with other than the twins and other nomads? Where did the diamonds originate? Who purchased his diamonds? Where is the money trail? What other items did he distribute?

Concerning the twins. They received and delivered diamonds, but who set up the purchases? Where was the bulk of their money? How did they actually get their items out of the country? Who were their other partners?

Concerning Bilal. Was he secretly involvement? How did we upset their operation? I never purchased souvenirs and Bilal never agreed to make deliveries…or did he?

Concerning Lizette. Why was she kidnapped? Was she really kidnapped? Is she really involved in khat transporting or is she transporting something else? Diamond perhaps? Should I try to confront her or should I leave it alone?

More questions. Who shot Na'im? Who shot the ones who shot at us? Are the Prime Minister or maybe even the Ambassador involved?

While loading the Roadie, the Prime Minister summons the Ambassador, Bilal and myself. "Gentleman, I would hope that the findings of today go no further and that the same would be expressed to your people as it will be expressed to mine. I will meet you at the Royal Guard Headquarters."

Agreed.

•••••••••••

221

Paranoia was my only friend. I don't know who to trust and everyone is a suspect including those in this vehicle. I'm losing focus. Getting weary.

While in the trailer we also learned that Na'im's motto was "Service with a smile." Hence the yellow smiley sticker.

Reclining to nap the words of Bobby McFerrin soothe me, *"Here is a little song I wrote. You might want to sing it note for note. Don't worry. Be happy."*.

TWENTY-NINE

Tuesday, June 5, 2007, 7:40 P.M.

A Royal Guardsman motions for us to enter through the open gate of the fortressed compound. "We've been expecting you." Two Guardsmen on a golf cart take the Ambassador, Brokenbow and myself to the heavily guarded building called "*Idaara*" or "Administration". The others remain with the Roadie which is being directed to park near the armoured trucks.

We are escorted down two flights of stairs. Underground. Passing the morgue on our way to the detention area the Ambassador requests, "Let me see the dead man?"

Two Guards are readied at the door. They step aside. The actual morgue is much like a walk-in freezer. The door is opened. The physician removes his rubber gloves and extends his right hand. Smiling. "Doctor Robert Savant." I remember him as Billy from the Meeting having sat at the table with him during a few hands of Blackjack. His not being a Muslim allows him to attend

to the body on the gurney without being spiritually contaminated..
The body is face down displaying an entry hole through the back.
He is obviously a white male.

The Ambassador makes an interesting request, "Doctor,
can you turn the body so that I can see the face." He obliges. The
Ambassador remains stoic as he realizes that it is Wilhelm, the
owner of the *CJ Triskett*, the host of the Meeting. The man in the
black tux. A gaping hole displays where the bullet exited his chest.

The Ambassador asks Doctor Savant, "What can you tell
me?"

In a matter of fact manner the doctor explains, "This man
was shot at close range. No more than a few meters. The bullet
entered his lower back, then traveled upward and exited here,
through the upper left side of the chest. Looks like the effects of a
powerful handgun."

"Thank you Doctor."

Exiting the freezer, a Guard hands The Ambassador the
passport and ID that was found on the deceased. "Alexander
Camp. Akron, Ohio."

The Prime Minister enters the room. "It appears that we
have all been made to look foolish."

We walk down the hall to an observation room attached to
the Interview Room. Inside is Ulysses from the Meeting. The
other man in a tux. Alone. He is handcuffed and shackled and has

a bandage over his left shoulder. He is wearing orange prison pants. No orange shirt would appareantly fit his large muscular upper body so he wears a white tank top t-shirt. Wife beater. He's a big boy. Solid.

The Ambassador looks at Ulysses passport and mumbles aloud, "Real name is Henson Perry from Kansas City, Kansas."

The Ambassador and the Prime Minister enter the Interview Room. Brokenbow and I observe through a one-way glass window in the observation room. Also in the room are two Guardsmen that are actively maintaining an impressive display of computers, monitors, surveillance cameras and dictation machines. One, Ahmed is taping the conversation and seems to be providing technical support. The other, Waleed is wearing a headset and is transcribing the conversation as it occurs. The intercom is on.

The Prime Minister begins, "This is an official inquiry and it is being audio taped and video taped. Do you understand?

Henson Perry nods and says, "Yes."

"Contrary to what you might think, you only have the right to tell the truth. Do you understand?"

Perry nods and repeats, "Yes."

"Your friend was shot through the back and the bullet exited through his chest. You were tested and were found not to have gunpowder on your hands. You were shot through the shoulder. The bullet coming from behind you. Just you and your dead friend were found at the site. No weapons were found. This does not have to take very long. I would encourage you to start by telling me everything you think I should know about your presence in Djibouti and your friend's death and then tell me how both of you were shot in the back by non-existing weapons." The Prime Minister then sits on the bench, reaches inside his suit pocket and removes a cigar. Perry (aka Ulysses) is watching intently. The Prime Minster places the cigar snipper to the closed end of the cigar and "snip". He then leans forward and speaks softly and clearly, almost in a whisper, "Despite what you might think, 'snip' is the sound your neck makes when your throat is cut." The Prime Minister sits back in his chair, tilts his head slightly to the right and leisurely lights his cigar. He puffs gingerly to create a temporary inferno and with the crown completely lit, he takes a long slow draw, then slowly exhales. He blows smoke in the face of Perry, who begins coughing uncontrollably.

Perry recovers and wipes the tears from his eyes causing his chains to rattle. The look on his face shows some indication that the tension in the small room, the heavy smell of a good cigar, the stares of the Ambassador standing in the corner with arms folded are having an impact but he says nothing. Silence. The kind of silence that can only to be broken by an honest confession.

Perry breaks, "I didn't kill Alex."

Prime Minister, "Start at the beginning."

"We were at the Meeting on the *CJ Triskett*," Perry begins, "but we are not the owners of the ship."

"Continue."

"We were hired to play as if we were the owners."

"Who hired you?"

"We only know him as Baker."

The Ambassador, whose demeanor during interviews is usually mellowed, quickly grows tired of Perry's lack of urgency for the current situation. He lunges from the corner and into the face of the shackled young man, "Two men are dead and you had something to do with their deaths! It is time for you start telling us everything you know about who, what and freakin' where! This situation is serious and this lousy ass attitude you have is really starting to piss me off! If I don't get some real information in the next five minutes I'm leaving. And when I leave, you will be tried and executed for the killings of Na'im, and your friend, Alexander Camp. Oh and by the way, when I walk out that door, your American status means nothing! Start telling us everything you know like your life depends on it…because it does!"

Having gotten a fresh perspective on the situation, Perry takes a deep breath, "Alex and I met in the Navy. We kinda stayed in touch after we both got out. Still trying to see the world, we got temporary jobs working at a winery in Bourdeaux, France. The pay was crappy, the perks were alright, but the place was beautiful.

Like I said though, it was a temporary job and before leaving we were confronted by a man who called himself Baker. He asked if we wanted to work odd jobs for him and his business partners. We didn't ask a lot of questions because 'yes' was gonna be the answer anyway. Basically we were gonna work for only a couple of months make some fast money then move on. All we did was do odd jobs on merchant ships. Baker said his partners owned different vessels, so all we did was learn the different jobs on a ship and get paid. We were like, constant journeyman, yeah that's it. Apprentices y'know? Usually you'd get your ass kicked if you showed up on another man's vessel trying to be a part of the crew, but they were the owners so we were protected. We worked on ships in Portugal, Morocco, South Africa and Australia. Can I have some water?"

The Prime Minister snaps his finger and a Guardsman named Abrar opens the door and delivers bottled water immediately then exits.

The exhaling Prime Minister then asks, "How long did you work for Baker?"

"We started working for him a year and a few months ago. The money was good. Real good. The work was hard tough, but somehow Baker got us in and out before it became too much. He would pay us by putting money to our debit accounts. We did the work he put the money on the card. We really didn't have to spend much because everywhere we worked we stayed in decent places and everything was paid for. All we did was save a little, and spend a lot. Mostly on women, drinking and gambling. Y' know."

Ambassador, "Did you ever wonder why we two were picked for such a cushy situation?"

"We each might have wondered at some point, but we didn't care, and we didn't talk about it. It was too good. We just didn't want it to end. We had just finished a month and a half job in Australia. Then we got word that he had a big job for us in Djibouti, Africa. No big deal really. It was all about gettin' paid. He said that this time we would have to act like we owned the ship for a big special event. That really didn't bother us. Then he said that the owners and the ship are from Australia and we would have to use Australian accents. He sent us some tapes by a foreign language company called Rosette Stine, or something like that, but we didn't really need the tapes because the Aussie accent is like English with a twist. Besides, we had just come from *down under*. To be honest, we just watched Paul Hogan as *Crocodile Dundee* over and over again. It did the job, y'know. So, from the time we got on the plane in France we were Australian. We talked Australian. We walked Australian. We dressed Australian. Hell, we probably even smelled Australia, whatever that means. We had to change connections in Ethiopia and believe me the Aussie accent was working with the ladies. We connected flights and we arrived at the Djibouti International Airport and take a taxi to the Kempinski Palace Resort. Nice place, if you haven't been there you outta check it out. When we got there we were each given a note that instructed us to remain in our rooms until Baker arrived. We got there in the morning and he arrived around six that evening. He showed up with clothes and a tuxedo for each of us. Real nice stuff y'know. Shoes, shirts the works."

"What day did you arrive?"

"It was Thursday. Ethiopian Airlines. We touched down around a little after the noon hour."

"How did Baker communicate with you?"

"Usually by temporary cell phones. Phone carriers ain't really reliable internationally, so he would give us temporary cell phones from the area we were in. Other than that he used email. While we were here, we were instructed to stay with the itinerary. Oh, I almost forgot that in the room on the beds there were two phones, but they were more like walkie-talkies than cell phones. Close range to be sure we was connected to one another."

"Anything else."

"Yeah. This time was different because Baker was there with us for the first time."

The Ambassador asked, "You mean Baker was with you here in Djibouti?"

"Yes sir. He met us in South Africa, made sure our room situation was set, but he didn't stay. In Australia, he met us and instructed us to learn the people and the culture. Then he left. Here was the first he met us. Hell he actually took us to the *CJ Triskett*. It really didn't look like much on the outside. It just looked like a big rusty ol' cargo ship, nothing fancy. But then we went down into the cargo area, and oh my goodness. We couldn't believe it! It was like Vegas or Atlantic City inside a big ass boat! We were given a tour of the vessel topside, cargo hull, stem to stern. We met the crew and they treated us like the owners, because they didn't really know who the owners were. Fact is, a lot of cargo ships are owned by corporations, a few of 'em are owned by the ports they transport goods from so the idea of an owner serving as Captain is kinda fading. For us though, our job here was to act like the owners of the *CJ Triskett* and to be the host at the Meeting. I have to admit that the briefing that Baker gave us really didn't warn us of who would actually show up and how big this thing really was. The cars, the money, the staff. It was impressive. Y'know.."

The Ambassador asks, "At the Meeting, why did your friend lie about seeing the girl in the light blue and black dotted dress in the back of the van?"

"Oh that? Alex had mentioned to me that he heard the conversation about a lady at your table and it sounded like the lady we saw on Sunday. Now, I told him not to get involved but he kinda wanted to clear his conscience, I guess. Knowing we didn't do anything to help the lady."

The Prime Minister needed clarification, "Help who?"

"The lady in the light blue dress with the black dots. It was like this, Baker wanted us to make a purchase of some priceless souvenirs from some African guys. The dudes were twins. Right there on the side of the road, not far from the port. We spent $110,000 for two creepy lookin' white goat heads covered in salt. All we knew was that Baker said they were priceless, but we didn't give a damn because it was his money. Y'know. When they opened the door to the van there was this lady tied up and sitting in the back on the floor, but all we did was conduct business and leave. It was like she wasn't even there. We kinda felt crappy afterward, y'know?"

The Ambassador seemed unimpressed, "Yeah, good to know you got a conscience. Continue."

"Baker and his partners had everything covered. During the Meeting, we didn't deal with the money, because the Banking Supervisor was responsible for that. We didn't have to be concerned with the cleanup, cause the staff handled that. The Head Chef handled the kitchen area. The Ship's Foreman handled the vessel. Somebody else was in charge of all the girls. And security was handled, pretty much, by everyone who was invited.

Hell, everyone had some kinda bodyguard or personal protection. Our job was to act like the owners. Make sure everyone had a good time." He stops, "Can I have some more water please?"

Guard Abrar delivers two bottles. Perry opens one and guzzles the contents without stopping.

The Prime Minister persists, "What then?"

"Well, we were scheduled to fly out earlier today at 12 noon. Then Baker got a phone call, and everything started going crazy."

He downs the other bottle.

"Keep talking."

"When the Meeting was over we were called and instructed to meet Baker at Pier 17. He would pick us up."

"Wasn't he at the Meeting?"

"No Sir, and if he was I didn't see him. He stayed in touch with us through the short-wave walkie-talkies. We were originally instructed that a car would be coming to pick us up and take us to the hotel. We were scheduled to go back to the room, check out, and get to the airport. That morning, while we were in the room, Baker calls and tells us to meet him at Pier 17. It was around nine in the morning and we had just gotten in after leaving the ship and making sure that the ladies were escorted off. Everything else that was on the ship, left with the ship. Around nine fifteen he calls us on the radio and tells us to come down right away. He is in the front waiting and picks us up in a Ford F150 and says, 'The itinerary has changed. Get in!' We get in the truck and he's in a hurry, but outside of the Port gate we had to slow down because of something going on at some warehouse. We're thinking, 'No big deal, right?' But Baker starts cussing and hitting the steering wheel y'know. Usually he's all cool and smooth like, but whatever was going on at the warehouse must have been serious because there were guards outside wearing the same kinda uniforms that they wear here."

"You mean Royal Guard Uniforms."

"Yes Sir. Flashing lights were everywhere, y'know. Baker was really pissed at what he saw, and I could tell he didn't want to but he slowed down and kept going. Lookin' straight ahead y'know. After that we went to a place called the Market Square and got some breakfast at a French place. Baker got a call. Next thing you know, we were at a used car lot. He stayed in the truck but he instructed me to buy a car for three thousand dollars. He gave me the money. I did. I bought a blue ol' Dodge. It took no more than twenty minutes. Cash y'know. I stopped at a gas station to fill up, and Alex got in the car with me. Using the walkie-talkie Baker told us to follow him. We did and we ended up going to Lac Assal. On the way there we stopped and then he told us to block the road with the car we were driving. Then he gives Alex a sharp knife and tells him to slash the tires. After that we get in the truck, and he intentionally backs the truck up and rams into the side of the car. He then drove to where you found us, on the other side of the lake. He was blocking the other entrance with the ol' Dodge because he was hoping you guys would detour to the side that we was on."

The Ambassador presses, "Why did he want us on the other side of Lac Assal?"

"Well, me and Alex didn't know it at the time, but he had like, four rifles with scopes and a couple of handguns in the truck. I think he also had some hand grenades to be honest with you but he wanted you guys to come to the other side to be ambushed."

"Ambushed?"

"Yeah, he started mumbling about how this could happen, what to do next, kinda panicking, ya know. He said when they, meaning you guys, came that way we were to start shooting. Then, you guys show up on the other side in that black mobile home. Nice ride I gotta say. So he starts panicking and pacing around outside of the vehicle and mumblin'. 'What to do, what to do?' Then he tells us to kill the black guy, you know the African-American that was at the Meeting with you. There was a ridge on that side and Baker couldn't get up to take the shot, so he gave us each a rifle and he told us to take the shot. The ridge was too tall so I set the rifle down, and Alex stood on my shoulders. He was up there for more than a few minutes and my shoulders started shaking. Then from out of nowhere a helicopter comes in. We shoulda' left, but Baker insisted that we take the shot and kill the black guy. Like I said, my shoulders started shakin' y'know, Alex took the shot, and then there was a gang of bullets that came our way. While the bullets were coming at us and while he was still on my shoulders, Baker asked, 'Look through the scope. Did you get him?' Alex said, 'No. It looks like I shot the old African wearing the skirt.' Well, Baker didn't like that information and got pissed. I kinda glanced back and saw that he had pulled out the handgun, pointed it at us then said, "Useless!" He shot Alex in the back. I jumped for my rifle I had set down and he shot me in the back, more like in the shoulder. I fell down and played dead. I was glad I went facedown, cause the shots from the other side were serious. I even felt two bombs explode. Sand and salt and stuff was flyin' everywhere. Damn! That was scary. I was kinda able to squint and see what Baker was doin'. He didn't take cover. He didn't even respond to the bombs goin' off. He simply bent down and got our rifles, got in his truck and left us there. I didn't know that Alex was dead cause I was too afraid to move. A few minutes later the Guard had a gun to my head ordering me to get up."

"Anything else?"

"Well…there is one thing that kinda started to creep me out."

"Go on."

"Well…I like women. Alex liked women. Y'know. But every once and a while Baker would, like, shake your hand and hold it a few seconds too long and kinda look into your eyes. Creeped me out, y'know. Before we left from the French café after breakfast this morning, he touched my face with the back of his hand. Real soft like. That kinda stuff just ain't right. Creeped me out. Matter of fact I think that's why Alex got in the car with me after I bought it. Just creepy. Y'know?"

The Prime Minister quips, "Thank you for the information you have so willingly shared, but we are just getting started."

Questions are coming at Perry at a more rapid pace. He drinks more water. Some of the questions have already been answered, but are back for an encore. Clarification. Illumination.

"So you said…?"

"Are you sure…?"

"What time was it when…?"

"How much…?"

The description Perry gives of Baker made him look like any other healthy, brown-eyed, middle-aged, white, French speaking male, average height, average weight with a full head of dark hair and a mustache. No glasses. No tattoos. No other distinquishing characteristics. He generally wore dark shades. No rings. No speaking peculiarities. No noticeable movement oddities. Vanilla.

Two hours had elapsed. Q & A. The interrogation ended with Perry, still shackled at the wrist and the ankles, shuffling down the hall to a holding cell where two Guards stand watch.

The Ambassador looks at the Prime Minister, "What do you think?"

"I think he was telling the truth. His answers were consistent." Thinking twice, the Prime Minister comments, "It sounds as if he got himself into something that he was not expecting. What do you think about Baker?"

The Ambassador hesitates, thinking of the right words, "I think Baker does exist. At first I thought it was a diversion, but the more he talked the more it made sense that someone else was in charge. But why would he want Dunstin dead?"

"I don't know but we do agree that Baker lives."

•••••••••••

At 10:35 P.M., Brokenbow sends for Bilal and I. We enter the interrogation room and are hit with the stale reminder of the smoke cloud that recently permeated the air. We talk freely, each knowing that the conversation was being recorded.

The Ambassador appears agitated, "Baker had to be on that ship. It would be nice to have the ship's guest list, but it doesn't exist because the damn ship was never in port!"

238

Brokenbow adds, "Either Baker truly has this country well researched or he's been here long enough to know his way around. Perry and Camp didn't know about Lac Assal, and they definitely didn't know that they would be shot."

The technical Guardsman Ahmed enters the room with large photos. "Sir, based on the information provided during your questioning we have developed a time line for Perry and Camp and their possible times with Baker. We are awaiting verification of their arrival time at the airport. Our surveillance lines are linked so we checked the surveillance cameras at Kempinski, the cameras at the Port, along with the four cameras in the Market Square, facing the French eating district. Each has images of Perry and Camp and possibly a third man."

The Prime Minister, unsatisfied, asks, "What do you mean possibly?"

Handing the Prime Minister the photos, "Sir, the other person either has their face covered or they are looking in the opposite direction when they are approximately twenty meters from the camera. Basically, the zoom bears no recognizable image. Most strangely is the fact that when they are within that twenty meter range the cameras become blurry. Distorted. Though I think it's a male, with these distortions we really can't tell if the third person is male or female."

That was something I did not want to hear.

The Prime Minister passes the photos to the Ambassador, then to Brokenbow, who studies them carefully and lays them out on the table. Ahmed comments, "Sir, it appears that Baker has some sort of a portable jamming devise. High tech stuff. He has tapped into our surveillance camera frequency and when he is within range, here's the effect."

The Prime Minister wearily looks at the Ambassador, "Baker is in my country, and I don't like it. Each of you, take down my personal phone number, 64-3785. Put it in your phones. Call me with anything *uncustomary* as it relates to this, Baker."

The Ambassador asks me, "Why does he want you dead?"

The Prime Minister asks, "Who might we have offended?"

Another hour passes as Bilal and I answer questions but are getting no closer to an understanding as to why someone would attempt to kill a low profile Professor from a Historically Black University in Atlanta, Georgia.

Throughout the investigation I never volunteer the information about Lizette being tied into something dirty but I grow more and more convinced that her dealings have something to do with the contract that was taken out on my life. She is the only connecting link but I need to talk with her first. Alone.

I owe her that.

I also owe it to myself.

THIRTY

Wednesday, June 5, 2007, 12:19 A.M.

Bilal departs in the Mitsu.

It is late and each of us is exhausted. I look forward to finally getting some sleep. The wear and tear of being on the move at such a high pace for the last three days is showing as my entire upper body begins to sink down into my chest. Adrenaline and fear had been my diet, but I also tried a cup of Ethiopia's finest brew and I too can attest to its ability to make the goats jump.

The Ambassador and I get out of the vehicle and walk to the side door of the house while the Agents take the Roadie through it's normal systems check before shutdown. Entering the door, the Ambassador whispers, "They need not know of today's events. Hooah."

"Understood. Hooah."

The door opens and Emmie comes running to hug her husband. She is followed by Lizette and Sahar. Each bouncing with excitement like little children right before the presents are about to be opened. I am surprised by the welcoming embrace that I received from both Lizette then Sahar.

Before going further, Sahar jumps into my arms a second time and kisses me on the cheek. "Thank you."

"Is something going on that I don't know about?"

Lizette couldn't contain her excitement, "Earlier in the day and started talking about who we are and how we came to be in the kitchen together at that moment in time. Girl stuff, ya know? Emmie told us about her and the Ambassador."

Sahar echoes, "Such a sweet story. So romantic."

Lizette continues, "I told them about you and I and about how you left me to catch a taxi the first time we met."

"You did what?"

"It's a long story Ambassador."

Lizette continued, "But the amazing part was when Sahar started telling us about her experience, growing up in Giyon and being taken from her family. She also told us about some money you gave her for a special purpose."

I whisper to Sahar, "Is that all you told them?"

She winks. "You might want her to finish."

Lizette continued, "When Emmie heard what Sahar had been through she said, 'Get the money we're going downtown to pay a debt.' You would have thought we were crazy but we went downtown to the club and asked for Marco, the owner. He was the one who owned her papers."

Emmie high fives Sahar. Giddy.

Lizette continues, "You should have seen him as he stood there with three women, having just stepped out of a Lincoln Continental with Embassy plates, and Sahar steps to him and shows him $11,000 cash. She counts the money in front of him. He snorts, 'Where you gonna go, hookin' is all you know.' Then Emmie stepped in front of him and said, 'She deserves your respect, and you will give it!' She's looking at him eye to eye, then she says to Sahar, 'Sweetie, go get your things. You don't belong here anymore!'"

Impressed the Ambassador asked, "You did that honey?"

Emmie responds, "I'll say, I was on my tiptoes the whole time."

"Yes she did! She was *magnifique!*" Lizette and Sahar, high five.

Lizette proceeds, "Marco went to his office and came out with two pieces of paper. He sat down and took the time to fill in the necessary information. When Sahar came back downstairs, he signed them in her presence. Then Sahar signed. Stamped on each of the papers were the words DEBT PAID!"

The ladies couldn't contain themselves as they embraced and jumped and cried and celebrated.

Emmie then picks up the story, "But that wasn't the end of it, when Sahar went to give Marco the money, he said, 'I heard you had something to do with getting the twins off the streets. I hear one is dead because of you. We've all wanted those two taken out since they killed that kid in the alley. On second thought, Keep your money. We even. I didn't mean what I said earlier, you're a good girl. Your debt is paid and if anybody's got a problem you tell em' to come see Marco.'" The outburst could not be contained, this time we all join in the celebration.

Sahar kisses me on the cheek. "Thank you for what you did for me."

She then kisses me on the other cheek, "Thank you for what you did for Maxi and the kids."

I ask, "How long have you known about me and the children?"

She explains, "Djibouti City is small. Good news travels fast and some of the kids you helped were related to the ladies I worked with."

Coyly Emmie asks, "Ambassador, being that we are stopping in Addis later today, can we take Sahar back to Ethiopia?" She then lays her head on his chest. *"Please."*

The Ambassador thinks aloud, "It's against everything in the book, but after you all went through the trouble of scaring the hell out of a guy named Marco, I guess it wouldn't hurt."

Emmie holds her excitement, "Is that a yes?"

"Yes."

The three started jumping and bouncing with joy all over again. It was worth it. Sahar, a free woman, was going home.

The Ambassador halted the celebration, "Wait! She's gonna need a passport."

Emmie responded, "Oh that's alright baby, we stopped by the Prime Minister's residence and I visited his wife. She understood. The paperwork was completed today. We pick up the passport in the morning. Official State business, you know?" Emmie salutes.

"Come here you." They hug and kiss.

At that I had to jump in, "Now that's a happy ending. It's time for me to get some sleep. Sahar, congratulations kid. You deserve it. Emmie, Ambassador, you deserve one another and I will forever be in your debt. Lizette I'm glad you're safe. We'll talk tomorrow. Good night everyone." While walking up the stairs I ask, "What time do you plan to leave for the airport?"

Emmie responds, "Twelve noon. Breakfast is at seven."

"Okay, good night, see you at six fifty-nine."

After showering I sit on the edge of the bed, thinking about the events that have transpired. Taking it all in, I kneel down beside the bed and begin to pray. "Thank you, Lord! Thank you, Lord! Thank you, Lord!"

I climb onto the bed and lay my head on the pillow.

Out.

THIRTY-ONE

Wednesday, June 6, 2007, 6:57 A.M.

Seated at the table along with myself are the Ambassador, Emmie, Sahar and Lizette.

The staff begins service at the sound of the seven o'clock gong from the grandfather clock. Top of the hour. The unwritten rule is that if Emmie told you when breakfast, lunch or dinner would occur, it wasn't a suggestion. Be seated and ready to eat.

The relationships and the experiences among those around the table create the feel of a family reunion. Interestingly, none of us really knows the other, save for the host couple, but there is a bond we now share that will never be broken. The last few days have made us like family.

I try to image what the persons around the table might be thinking. Emmie is all smiles because she loves to entertain and she truly seems to be enjoying the visitation of her special new friends.

Initially, I concerned about Sahar, but her bright and beautiful smile lets me know that she was well rested and was looking forward to changes in life. She seems hopeful and her excitement could not be masked and why should it, she was going home today. I realize that she didn't know what to expect, but I am sure that any place would be better than where she had been.

The Ambassador and I sat at opposite ends of the table but it didn't stop us from laughing and talking. Nothing serious and no mention of the most recent events. It felt good to enjoy these light-hearted moments with someone who had been there with you.

I watch as Lizette becomes the social darling that has helped to garner her a professional reputation of efficiency with pleasantness. Of the time we've spent together, this was the first in which I was able to be with her in a larger setting with others. I glance across the table and notice her easy ways, the delicate gestures of her hands, the movement of her lips when speaking, and the warmth I experience when she laughs. Affable. She does not appear to be traumatized by the recent happenings, only motivated. I listen as Emmie asked Lizette if she would stay at the house while they were gone. She agreed.

Me. I was just glad to get some sleep.

After the main course of a delicious breakfast, there was a momentary lapse as the staff cleared the table. The pause lasted no more than a few minutes, but the reality for each of us was probably much different than our outer countenance.

•••••••••••

Emmie. *"I don't how much longer I can take this. I saw his bloodied shirt in the trash. Trousers with holes in the knees as if he'd been in a scuffle. I'm tired. We have been together to damn long and we are getting to damn old for this Super Soldier act to continue. I am tired of praying for the safety of a man who cares little for the same. For too many years I waited by the phone. Waiting, but not wanting, to receive that call. I appreciate the places and the adventures but it is time to wind down and he still finds ways to test the limits. I waited by phone through Grenada, Desert Storm, Mogadishu and all during the covert missions that he doesn't think I know anything about. He doesn't seem to take seriously the fact that he is an American Ambassador and he is a target. I just wish he would consider that when he leaves the compound by himself in that raggedy ass white car."*

•••••••••••

Sahar. *"I hope they will take me back. The stories of girls that were taken from their homes and not able to return are too*

*many to count. I don't know what I would do if I got home and my
father turns me away. I have been abused and I have been hurt in
ways that are deep within my soul and I cannot describe my pain.
Now, I just want to go home. I just want that fifteen year old girl
to find a place to lay her head without being afraid. I had to kill a
man to get what was taken from me. I shot him in the head the
same way I say the elders do to dogs that have rabies. One bullet
right between the eyes. No remorse."*

••••••••••••

Ambassador. *"The last few days have been great. The
excitement. The action. I am back in the saddle. I just regret not
knowing for how long. The doctors haven't said anything that was
conclusive and I don't want to alarm Emmie. Some other time.
Something about the Prime Minister leaves me uneasy. I'll deal
with it some other time. To the States!"*

••••••••••••

Lizette. *"I didn't sleep well. I can't believe that my life
was is danger. I haven't done any harm to anyone. I try to treat
people right. I wonder if my past is coming back to haunt me.
I've never met a man like Carter. He is good and kind. He turns*

250

me on. I just wonder if he can help me to maintain my standards for travel and business? Will he support my habits? Will he support my extra ways of earning a living or will he have a negative mindset to what might become a lucrative future for the both of us? I hope he's open-minded, but if not, I'll do without him."

•••••••••••

"As tired as I was my sleep was hampered by the fact that someone was trying to kill me at Lac Assal. I've been beaten up and thrown into a pile of rotting death...literally. None of the recent revelations makes any sense to me. More importantly, I need to complete my research I need to know if my efforts are to pay off or if I've been wasting my time. Either way I need to move forward with my life, but before I can go forward I must confront Lizette with the possibility of her being involved in illegal activities that might bring more pain. Khat dealing is low but the possibility of the third person with Henson and Alex maybe being a woman. Hell no! Others have suffered and it needs to stop. I also got to live the rest of my life knowing that had I known that Boulos and Butrus were the one's who killed Maxi, I would have shot them myself. It's not over. Paranoia is still my closest companion. Can Bilal be trusted Damn.."

251

The momentary silence is broken by the swinging of the kitchen door as the staff continues service and lively conversation resumes.

I ask Emmie, "So you have to be at the airport at noon, but what time do you have to pick up the passport?"

"Passport pickup will be 9:30." To Sahar, "So have your stuff packed and downstairs by 8:30."

I take Sahar by the hand, "I had hoped to see you before you leave, but I may not have that chance so I want to tell you face to face that you are the strongest and most intelligent young woman I have ever met. I have always seen something special in you, and now you have the opportunity to fulfill your dreams and live life on your terms. Whatever you do and wherever you go, I encourage you to never let the painful past drag you down. You are special. I am very proud and honored to know you."

Her eyes swell to overflowing and the five year wall of protection begins crumbling. Tears flow. "Professeur, you saved my life. I will forever be in your debt."

With a smile, "If I am correct, you evened the score at the warehouse. I'm like Marco, *'Debt Paid.'* I might not be sitting here if it weren't for you. What do you think Ambassador?"

"Paid if full."

Emmie asks, "Sounds like you won't be coming with us to the airport?"

"No ma'am, I've got to get back to my work."

The Ambassador asks, "Don't you think it's a little early for that Dunstin? Shouldn't you wait until given the all clear?" He leans toward me and whispers, "Someone is trying to kill you, you know?"

"Ambassador, I'm a scientist and I'm very close to finding something and I don't know what that something is, but at this point my research is the only thing keeping me sane. Basically…" I lean toward him and whisper, "If I don't get back to my work, I'm dead already."

"Suit yourself soldier. The wife and I will be back in two weeks, and we would be honored if you and Lizette would join us at the Independence Day Celebration on the 27th of June. This year will mark the 30th year of Djiboutian independence from the French and it promises to be a memorable event."

"We would be honored Sir."

"Dammit Dunstin, there you go with that Sir crap again."

Laughter, "Have a good trip Ambassador, and with all seriousness, thank you for all that you and Emmie have done for me, Lizette, Sahar, and Bilal." Handshake. Manhug, complete with back slapping.

Gutteral, "Hooah!"

"Hooah!" He winks. Exits.

I kiss Emmie on the cheek, "Have a good trip." She then motions to Sahar, "Come upstairs honey and take some of the clothing from the closet for her return."

Sahar and I hug. Maybe for the last time. "Be good kid." I kiss her on the forehead. "Remember, don't look back." She turns and goes upstairs.

As they ascend, "Oh yeah, ah, Emmie is it alright if I visit Lizette here while you're gone."

"It's alright to visit. Just remember, no sleeping in the same bed if you stay over night. We're Republicans."

"Yes ma'am."

Lizette pulls me close, "I cannot thank you enough for all that you have done for me. I know we have experienced a lot in a very short period of time and I think I've really falling for you Carter Dunstin. If that scares you, come back later and we'll talk about it. If it does not scare you, then just come back later."

Now! Now! Now! Now is the perfect time to share my concerns with Lizette about the allegations made against her. *Just get it over. Ask her. She'll deny it. It's done. Move on. No big deal. Just get it over.*" Standing there, looking into the wonder of her big brown eyes, my mouth can only utter the words, "I'll be at the University. I'll come by later." We kiss.

Holding one another she comments, "I've noticed that you haven't been as affectionate towards me lately. As a matter of fact, the last time you really hugged me was at the warehouse. Is there something you want to talk about?"

My mind is screaming to the degree that I thought she might have heard my thoughts. *"ASK HER! ASK HER! ASK HER!"* I open my lips to speak, but for now my thoughts will have to go unsatisfied, "We'll talk later." Light kiss.

A taxi is summoned. Another round of hugging. Armed with a loaded backpack I am ready for the success of a new day. WHEN I FIND WHAT ISN'T, IT WILL BE!

Headphones on. Michael puts it in perspective, *"Take a look at yourself then make the change."*

Make that change!

THIRTY-TWO

Wednesday, June 6, 2007, 9:10 A.M.

"Bonjour Professeur Dublé."

"Bonjour Professeur Dunstin."

I was eager to get back to my work and my intent was to exchange simple pleasantries and continue to the Zone. Therefore, I was caught off guard by the comment coming from Dublé. "Two days ago, I was attacked and I was most disappointed to have only heard from you once since my ordeal. I was beginning to wonder if I had lost a friend."

My father once told me that, *"Nothing is real unless it's personal."* I searched my mind to find that I had not told Dublé about the most recent events experienced by Bilal and myself and others. I don't think he was intending to be insensitive. He simply needed reassurance that in me, he had a colleague and a friend.

"Nonsense Dublé, my friendship is yours without fail and I must say that you are looking much better since I last saw you?"

"I'll do fine Professeur Dunstin, just remember that good relationships are hard to find. I do have classes and papers to grade so I'll leave you to your work." He moves towards me and touches my face in a way most uncommon…soft and gentle. Truly creepy. He then shuffles down the hallway with briefcase in the right and cane in the left.

"Relationship" seems a bit more than the appropriate terminology concerning the good Professeur and myself. "Did he just make a pass at me?" Self reasoning, "Naw, he's just French." Trying not to put too much thought into his unsettling display, I shrug it off, head straight for the Zone and get down to business.

I dawn the disposable lab coat. The mask is in place. The headphones are on with NANO cranking the hauntingly spectacular sounds of Carl Orff's, *"O fortuna."* Latin heightening my senses, *"O fortuna. Velut luna. Statu variabilis."* It translates, *"Oh fortune, like the moon, you are changeable."* I've toiled at Lac Assal for the last seven months and today my fortunes shall change. Deep breath. I secure my weapons for battle. Spiral notebook and blue *BIC*. Digital camera and cassette recorder. Deep breath. Like a gladiator entering the arena and readied for battle, I am here! Today I will change my fortune!

Inside are me and my destiny. The blinds remain closed. The door is locked from the inside. The purpose is psychological, "I'm not leaving until I find what isn't."

I briefly look over my notes. Artificial sunlight had been set to stay on for twelve hours. 7 A.M. to 7 P.M. The temperature settings were the high of 120° Fahrenheit and the low of 80° Fahrenheit. The control side of the experiment also included the chicken carcass that has not been touched since Saturday. Deep inhale. Slow exhale. Before removing the black covering from the observation enclosure, I think about the whirlwind of events over the past few days. My routine has been altered and my relationship with the important people in my life have been repositioned. I pause, then say the words from the old Negro Spiritual, *"Guide my feet Lord, while I run this race. I don't want to run this race in vain."*

Not knowing what to expect, I nervously remove the black cloth.

"Oh my goodness. Oh my goodness!"

I manage to insert a blank cassette tape into the cassette player and press the record button. "Oh my goodness." I grab for the camera, making sure that the mode is set to video and begin filming while narrating. "The date is Wednesday, June 6, 2007. The time is 9:43 A.M. Right now, it is difficult to contain my excitement. Hoping that there might be a few living specimen to consider, I am now looking at hundreds of flies inside the glass examination dome. HUNDREDS! The chicken retrieved from Lac Assal Site III is nothing but a carcass. There are no obvious remnants of meat remaining on the chicken. Hanging on the bones, are what look like new larva, but for now I will classify them as an unidentified feeder that is much smaller that the original fly larva. Most of the flies are resting, seemingly bloated from the meal consumed. Many of the flies are exhibiting pregnant flying patterns. Here too, I must take into consideration that the enclosure has limited their normal flying abilities. Oddly, the flies are clustering in the corners of the enclosure, some on top of others, but they don't appear to be mating or attacking. The rocks are hosting a few maggots and new larvae. The salt rock is clear of the flies, the maggots, and the larvae. I must also note that I am unfamiliar with what I am observing. I have never seen anything like the fly specimen enclosed. I will proceed with Protocol three through seven."

I remove one fly from the enclosure. It is then frozen with the spray.. Photographed. Examined. Dissected.

I continue filming their behavior. "Note that there does not appear to be an order of leadership and or servitude. Each appears to be working to ensure their own survival." I expected a few specimen to be post-larva, but this is exceptional. To find them in the pupae stage would have been amazing, but to find fully developed and functioning flies is extraordinary. Flies generally don't have an infant to adult growing period. They emerge from the pupae stage as fully functioning adults."

The basic reasoning behind the format of my research and the location of Lac Assal has been fourfold:

- One, due to the heat and the barren nature of the topography, the Lac Assal region has remained largely unexamined, and or under-examined.

- Two, for the same reasons supporting number one, the Lac Assal region has remained largely undocumented concerning its local or indigenous insect and animal life.

- Three, the Insecta Class has more undocumented species than any other in the Animalia Kingdom, to wit, I reason that new species will be found at Lac Assal.

- Four, depending on the existence and the patterns of the new find it must be determined if the new find adds to human/animal benefit or to human/animal suffering. Research then attempts to sustain or to eradicate.

My focus in Lac Assal has been in the Order of *diptera* which is flies or mosquitoes, along with *siphonaptera* (fleas) and *strepsiptera* (parasites). Hypothetically, the chicken was intended to draw the attention of insects that are indigenous to the area. The conditions in the Afar Depression are so severe that the list of

261

insects is comparatively small because of the harsh conditions. That is not to say that insects cannot thrive there, but that is to say that to do so, over time, they must evolve and oftentimes become creatures only loosely favoring their ancestors. The process of adapt and overcome.

I can't escape the comparison of the limited variety of insects at Lac Assal as compared to the blight of samples introduced to me at the bone yard. One has so few and the other has an abundance. Though pained, disoriented, and basically wanting to breathe freely the experience in the Valley of Death was not without its scientific merit. I've been here for almost seven months and working with blinders on. It never occurred to me that the waste management techniques of a people, or the lack thereof, could serve as the basis for my research. My focus was reserved for Lac Assal, and its harsh conditions, and basically I was missing the forest because I was too focused on the trees. The focus should have been Djibouti, not just Lac Assal! It's Biology 101 and I missed it. Too simple.

Wherever there are humans, past and present, there is always a need to answer the pivotal question, "How do or, did they dispose of their waste?" Social structure and intellect is detailed in the ways that people have, and do dispose of waste, both bodily and material. While excited about what I see before me, I can't fight the notion that I must return to the site in the "Valley of dry bones," and under more controlled circumstances, I would enjoy the opportunity to have the caretaker and his family interviewed and tested. How long have they been there? What exactly are his responsibilities? How is he paid? Is he paid? How have their bodies adapted to their surroundings, or are they slowly dying of disease?

Without warning I burst out in song with Aretha "The Queen of Soul" Franklin, *"R-E-S-P-E-C-T. Find out what it means to me. R-E-S-P-E-C-T. Take care of TCB. Oww. Sock it to me..."* It seemed appropriate.

I continue narrating as I capture another fly in the escape hatch. It is anesthetized and while immobile I take pictures. Easy to note are the unique markings on its brownish-blue wings and the wavy pinkish pattern on its large purplish eyes. The markings appear consistent with the other specimen. Most notable is the mouth. It has large brown fangs, with a relatively long and coiled black tongue. I then pin the specimen to the board for further examination. Pictures are taken as I continue to narrate and record my findings on the cassette player. Every stage of examination and the subsequent dismantling is documented in the notebook. Every stage is photographed. The photos are then uploaded to the computer and sent to my Department Chair, Dr. James Heggie, at Clarkmore University. I want him to know that these efforts are not in vain, and I need his assistance to help in the classification and verification process. Photos are also sent to the Convention of Insecta Taxonomist which is an International Body established to investigate and legitimize insect verification claims.

I research the internet for any comparable examples. None. Hours pass as I continue searching. I check the books in the lab for noted examples. None. Nothing on-line and nothing in the periodicals. I am getting excited. I keep in mind the controlled and contained element, but even so I am elated. I know that the final verification will come from my being able to duplicate the experiment at least seven times, with the same results. Though I recently thought of Lac Assal as a place to be avoided, I am encouraged in the notion that my work has not been in vain.

I scream, "ONCE I FIND WHAT IS, IT WILL BE! BABBBYYYY!"

The good news in the headphones heightens my feeling of celebration because it, *"Makes me clap my hands, makes me wanna dance and STOMP!"* Kirk Franklin, you're right on time!

•••••••••••

It's 6:35 P.M. on this, the best day of my career. I go to Dublés office to share some of the good news. Not all. Some. His door is opened, so I step inside. I sit in the chair and look around the room while recalling my high school days. I wait for a couple of minutes and return to the Zone.

I attempt to use my phone, but I don't get a signal until I wander down the hallway. I call Bilal. "My brother, it is time to celebrate. I have found something *uncustomary*. I know it is late, but get here PM. Room 318."

I return to the Zone, locking the door. The NANO is charging via the computer and the headphones are on the table. I insert a blank 120 minute cassette into the player and press the record button. "It will be necessary for Protocol three through seven to be instituted a second time on another specimen. The purpose…" I hear a knock at the window. Peaking through the blinds I see that it's Professor Dublé. He raises a bottle of Sherry and a bottle of Merlot.

I concede and return the black cloth to the enclosure. It is time to take a break. I remove the lab coat and the mask. I exit the Zone and leave the door propped open.

Holding two bottles, two glasses, and a paper bag, he shuffles to the table, "Professeur Dunstin, I came by earlier only to find you locked inside with blinds closed and I said to myself, 'He needs a break and a glass of inspiration.' Besides, no one else is in the building at this time, so I generally find it ripe for relaxation.

"I appreciate it Professeur Dublé. I did need a break and a glass of Merlot is a good way to re-focus. Thank you."

Filling my glass he asks, "Have you found anything interesting?"

I had resolved that Bilal will know about the latest progress before anyone else. I remained coy, "Everything is interesting, but I don't know if I have found anything promising."

"Well stated Dunstin. Well stated. A toast to finishing what was started." He raises his glass of Sherry and I the glass of Merlot.

He toast, "Here's to new horizons."

After a few minutes of lighthearted, but meaningless conversation I ask, "What time do you plan to leave this evening?"

He smiles, "Well, I'll be here most of the night."

Leaving the glass half full, I get up and walk toward the Zone. "Great. I'll keep you company."

"No, no, no Professeur Dustin. Sit. Let me tell you a story."

I sit in a chair near the open door to the lab. I vaguely attempt to hide my agitation with a weak smile. I am his guest. He is my friend. "Continue."

"Well, Professeur Dunstin, there comes a time when a man must examine who he is and what he has accomplished in life."

Trying to appear interested, I nod, "True, continue."

"From this point on Professeur Dunstin, don't say a damn thing, just listen."

The bluntness of his words landed like a sledge hammer to the face. Seething, I sit. Silent.

"Dunstin, I have stifled my brilliance. I have worked too damn hard to maintain a certain level of anonymity about my affairs and how I conduct my business. My façade as the humble and witless Professeur has served me well, but I am now at the point where I want others to know of my greatness."

Stone-faced, I sit. Arms folded. Leg crossed.

He continues, "I asked you specifically to stay away from Lizette, and instead of our friendship having any value you've taken the liberty to frolic."

Right now, this dude has gone waaaayyyyy over the line, but I manage to sit and say nothing.

"There are plenty of woman in Djibouti, hell most of them are your color, but you had to choose the one that I specifically asked you not to get involved with. I thought you were my friend. How do you think that makes me feel? Speak up for yourself dammit!"

"I don't know who in the hell you think you're talkin' to, but this…"

"Shut up!"

I begin to stand up.

"Sit down Dunstin." He pulls a handgun from his pocket and places it on the table. Smugly, "Sit down."

I oblige.

He stands and leans on the edge of the table. "Let me put it all together for you Professeur Carter J. Dunstin. For ten years I have served as a Professeur at this second rate institution, in this God forsaken country, and do you know why? It's because it has allowed me to get all that I want and more. I have respectfully served as an education professional, and you waltz your African-American ass in here and are close to an insecta find that will bring you international respect and professional credibility. Here's the rub, Professeur Dunstin, you won't get the credit. I will."

I can be disrespected as a person and continue to move forward without having to respond. I can be physically attacked and choose not to retaliate. This, however, was something new. For someone to talk of robbing me of fruits of this labor fueled an anger uncommon.

He picks up the handgun and leans forward, "Class is in session, so listen up. The twins, worked for me. They were my African pillars. Feel proud Dunstin, proud in knowing that I saw you as a worthy opponent. That's why I had Lizette kidnapped. Didn't you notice how she was abducted against her will but she was not harmed. If it were not because of my orders she might not be alive today. I am the one in control. Do you understand?! My orders kept her alive! MINE! Normally, the twins would have had their way with her, but they worked for me. They did what I told them to do! I am the puppet master. ME! And now, because of you, they have been taken away from me!"

I continue to sit and listen.

Gun in hand, he continues, "So far, you got my girl and you got my guys. The odds are in your favor. Your late night trip to the warehouse and then to the animal dump was to serve as a notice that you needed to leave Djibouti. Hell, I thought you would have gotten the hint when that little street urchin was beaten to death, back in March. For most, that would have been the last straw, but you seemed to be determined to stay."

"You had Maxi killed?!"

"It was more like…having him, stomped out of existence. Literally. Like an insect." Dublé begins to laugh.

Like a round from the chamber I leap across the room and hit Dublé squarely in the jaw. He falls back. I grab his throat and start choking him, and banging his head on the floor. "HE WAS JUST AN INNOCENT KID!" In my rage, clear thinking is abandoned. I feel the cold steel of the gun against my temple as he softly says, "I like it when you're angry." He winks. "What fun. Now get up!"

I bang the back of his head on the floor one more time, "Oops. My bad."

He places the barrel in the middle of my forehead, "Ohh, one more to remember you by, huh?"

Miffed, I get up and go back to the chair next to the open door of the Zone. I sit. Head in hands. "He was just a kid. He did nothing wrong to you or to anybody?"

Dublé stands and returns to leaning on the edge of the table, "Think about it Dunstin, after meeting Lizette I told you that she was not to be dealt with, but the day after you were sitting and enjoying her company at the Kempinski. You took something from me! So I took something from you! You took her so I took him. Makes perfect sense."

With clarity comes confusion, "She wasn't yours! He wasn't mine!"

He stands up, and starts pacing, "Technicalities! Shut up!" I notice he is not using the cane, nor is he bent at the back.

He continues, "You took my girl. And you took my guys. They were beautiful you know, with their coal black skin. They were beautiful and ruthless. Smooth and black. Same height. Strapping muscles. Same expressions. So beautiful. They were like panthers that would go on the prowl at my beckoning." He pauses and takes in a deep breath.

He lunges towards me, pointing the gun, "YOU TOOK THEM FROM ME!"

Reflex. I stand.

"SIT DOWN! I'M NOT DONE YET!" He grabs the paper bag that is sitting on the corner of the table. He reaches inside and pulls out a brunette men's wig with gray streaks, and a similar colored mustache.

Awestruck and jaw-dropped, "Baker."

He demands. "Say it with conviction, Henrì Dublé is Baker."

Taking it all in I comply, "Henrì Dublé is Baker."

Enjoying his new revelation, "You see Professeur, while you and your well-dressed Ambassador and the Prime Minister of this God-forsaken country were looking in all the wrong places Baker was operating out of Djibouti all along. Professeur Dublé is poor by worldly standards, but Baker is rich beyond your simple imagination. The cut diamonds in the salt crystal sculptures was my idea and it has worked to perfection for years…until you. I have been able to transport diamonds, cut and uncut, all over the world." He pauses for a moment of self-adulation. "Connecting with men to do my bidding has served me well. I was considering inviting you into to join me, but that consideration ended when you first walked Lizette to her flat. Pity. All of my men are paid to do what I tell them to do, but none of them actually knows how their actions fit into the big picture. Only I know the big picture! I am the puppet master! ME!"

He paces and talks as if he were on stage.

"This was the first time I got in on the Meeting at Pier 17, but I can guarantee you that it won't be the last. With money, I am able to pull the strings of anyone at anytime, but here again Dunstin, you took away my boys. My beautiful and obedient boys. My beautiful African boys. My beautiful American boys." He begins to whimper.

I remind him, "You shot two of them both in the back and left them for dead."

"Technicality! Shut up! As I was saying, I have been able to run rings around the Kimberly Process for diamond distribution, and for the record I don't care how much blood is shed by slaves, or children, or whoever, I just want my stones. Preferably uncut. Once I get rid of you, Baker will have to fade but he'll be back."

Still pacing, enjoying every moment, "This is the grand *fin*. I got in very early today and I checked your specimen in there. Very impressive. Quick investigation has me thinking that you have, at least, one new fly to claim, and maybe a new parasite. Sadly though, after all of the hours and the diligent months of study, the credit won't be yours. It will be mine. Following your soon disappearance, I am going to console Lizette. I will stroke her silky black hair like you did at the Kempinski. I will give her things, beautiful things, and soon you will be forgotten. What's more, I'm going to take Bilal from you and I'm going to hire him to take over where Na'im and the twins left off. Either way, I will pay him five times what you pay and he will come to remember you as another cheap American."

I interrupt, "Good to see you're healed. You don't have the limp in your walk and your left side isn't dragging."

Arrogantly he retorts, "Check the record Dunstin, my secondary major in school was Theatre."

I clap mockingly, "Bravo."

He gives a fake bow then orders, "So let's get started with the final act. Stand up!"

I oblige.

"Do you want to beg for the mercy of Dublé?"

As I stand here, I realize that I have absolutely nothing to lose. Maybe I have everything to lose, either way I couldn't hold my tongue, "Man, you out your damn mind and all that beggin' stuff, ain't gonna happin! People are dead because of your selfishness, and concerning Bilal and Lizette, mark my words I will haunt you. He is a good man. And she has done no wrong to anybody, except to love me when I allowed a pootbutt like yourself to cause me to doubt that love…and Maxi…man, I oughtta walk over there, take that gun out of your sweaty hand, and whoop yo' ass, but I got a feeling you like a good beatin' so do what you gotta do!"

He raises the weapon. Takes aim. "Silly American. Even worse, silly African-American."

"Nobody here to do your dirty work is it? You chalky white, bald head, French freak! Pull the damn trigger!"

I stand there, looking him eye to eye. Everything about him disgusts me. The slight flare of his nostrils. His corny shirt and bowtie combination. The glint of sweat on his balding white scalp. His eyes gray, cold and empty. Soulless. The more I look at him, the more I thought of the tenor of his irritating, French accented voice. Basically, he was pissing me off because he was holding me up from my research.

Again, the words came out before I had a chance to censure them, "Hurry up and shoot the damn gun, so I can get back to my work! Dumbass!"

Dublé vacillates. He drinks in the moment as his master plan is moving to fruition. A look of celebration brightens his countenance. "Checkmate." He roles his neck. "Shooting the boys at Lac Assal was easy because I didn't have to see their pretty faces. Despite the current impasse, I find you to be an exceptional researcher. That said, turn around. One shot, back of the head, you won't feel a thing."

"What's up with the drama? Just shoot dumbass!"

He hesitates, "*Mon frière,* turn around."

"I never figured you for a drama queen but then again, I never figured you as Baker. Forget all this talking…SHOOT DUMBASS! SHOOT!"

He smiles, "Queen? Flattery. I am in charge here Dunstin. This is my moment. Turn around Professeur."

I turn slowly, realizing that my thoughts aren't as clear as I would have assumed when the moment of death is at hand. Nothing redemptive. No lamenting the life I've lived. No revelation of...

BANG!

BANG!

Ears ringing.

I feel no pain.

Am I dead?

Heaven or hell, it looks rather familiar.

I turn around and see that the gun has dropped out of his hand and Dublé is slowly buckling at the knees. His slow fall downward reveals...Lizette.

She is standing in the doorway with a gun in her hand. Smoke oozing from its barrel.

Dublé finally makes it to the floor, his breathing and his actions display shock, not death. I kick his gun across the floor and bend down, "Dublé are you alright?"

He murmurs, "I can't feel my legs."

"Checkmate that, dumbass!"

Stepping on his fingers, I walk over to Lizette and she falls into my arms. I cradle her as we sit in the chair, "Are you alright?"

"I am now."

"How much did you hear?"

"Enough to know that calling a man with a gun a 'dumbass' is not the best way to stay alive."

We hear the pounding of footsteps running down the hallway. Knowing she just shot a man, she is jolted and stands up immediately.

It's Bilal with the Prime Minister and members of the Djiboutian Royal Guard.

Seeing Dublé laying in a growing pool of blood, the Prime Minister orders, "*UTlubu l-is'aaf*!"

Bilal calls out, "Professeur! Professeur!"

I ask, "Brother, what took you so long?"

"After I made sense of your request, I called the Prime Minister, but I first had to convince Numa that I wasn't going to get hurt. It took some time for persuasion, but here I am."

The Prime Minister takes over the conversation, "Professeur Dublé, the ambulance is on the way." He then instructs the Royal Guardsmen, "Watch this door. No one is to come in, or out, without my instruction." He then closes the door. Inside the classroom are Lizette, Bilal, Dublé, the Prime Minister and myself.

"Alright, Professeur Dunstin, before others arrive, I need to know what proof you have that Professeur Dublé is Baker."

In a weakened voice, Dublé adds, "There's no way you could have known."

I begin, "On the contrary Dublé, I have five reasons that point to you as Baker. Some of the reasons are mundane, some more elaborate. Alone, these are mere tidbits, of no consequence, but combined they weave a web of suspicion that leads directly to one person, you!"

Class is in session. "Point number one. When recounting her ordeal, Lizette described the concoction that rendered her unconscious as being 'sweet smelling'. It took me a little while to put it together, but in the office of the Professeur there are jars of different substances, one of them being, $CHCl_3$. It was created as an anesthetic agent, but was banned because of its unreliability and hideous side effects which is death. $CHCl_3$ is trichloromethane, commonly known as chloroform. I'm sure that I'd be able to prove that you made it in a laboratory, using tropical plants and the open drop method. Some say that chloroform is the element that is connected to the phrase, 'The sweet smell of death.' I say it was used to anesthetize Lizette when she was kidnapped.

"Point two. It was obvious that Lizette's containment was froth with personal care. Care that the twins were not able to provide having operated as homicidal robots basically incapable of remorse or feeling. To them, sex and killing was nothing but a tool to express power. Looking around the storage room made to serve as an apartment, I observed the spycam in the vent over looking the bed. Another was placed in the bathroom. She was there for your viewing pleasure. What tipped me off Dublé was the change of clothing you retrieved when you had the door replaced. Your fantasies involving women required disrobing. She get naked, you get happy. Your earlier statements lead me to believe that you also enjoy the touch of men. Masochistic perhaps. I'm sure that your computer hard drive will prove me correct…you perve."

Lizette comments, "Dublé if I hadn't shot you, I'd shoot you."

"Point three. On Saturday, June 2nd when I called from Lizette's disturbed apartment, you said you'd call when you got in the area. I checked my phone the following day while at Camp LeMonier, you never called. This would not have appeared odd, but you made such a pathetic point of reminding me that I didn't call after your fake assault. That would be considered, over acting.

"Point number four was obvious yet undetected until I entered your office earlier. Sitting there I got a glimpse of what you called, 'the big picture.' The 4' x 5' world map on your wall. Blue string and thumbtacks starting in France then to Portugal, to Morocco, to South Africa, to Australia and finally to Djibouti. Sound familiar Prime Minister? The American in your custody, Henson Perry, gave us information that Baker sent he and Alexander Camp to work on ships in Portugal, Morocco, South Africa and Australia. This is no coincidence. Also on the map are black strings that I am sure we will find to be smuggling routes for conflict diamonds."

Dublé utters, "It is all coincidence. None of this is true."

The Royal Guardsman reports from other side of the door. "Mister Prime Minister, the ambulance has arrived."

He responds, "Tell them to wait!"

"Oh, Mister Prime Minister, I almost forgot." I walk into the Zone and retrieve the cassette from the tape deck. "The fifth element of proof will be found on this cassette tape. I left the door open to my lab because the cassette player was recording his every confessionary word. It is all on tape Mr. Prime Minister."

Dublé reacts, "Damn you Dunstin!"

The Prime Minister motions for the door to be opened and the ambulatory medical personnel are allowed to enter. Dublé is tended to.

"Dublè I almost forgot. Concerning your acting skills, it would help if you kept the cane in the same hand when walking. It helps the performance when one is consistent."

The Prime Minister continues, "Well done Professeur Dunstin. I am impressed." He offers me a cigar. "Before I forget, Professor Henrì Dublé, I have the authority to inform you that you are under arrest for the attempted murder of Professeur Dunstin, the kidnapping of Lizette Moniette, and for your part in the deaths of Na'im and Alexander Camp. I would strongly urge that you prepare to deal with some international offences as well." He then speaks to the members of the Guard, "*Yuraaqib!*"

While being stabilized and readied for transport, Dublé remarks, "Professeur Dunstin, let me assure you that this isn't over."

"You're right, it isn't over. You played with the lives of innocent people. I find you to be a bully, a coward and your idea of friendship really sucks. Believe me Dublé, for Maxi's sake, it isn't over."

Dublé is stabilized and placed on the gurney and taken away.

The Prime Minister and I walk over to, and raise the window. We light up, looking down on the loading of Dublé into the ambulance. "One thing puzzles me Professeur, how did you alert Bilal without Dublé knowing?"

"You helped with that Prime Minister. When you gave us your personal number you said to call you if we found anything '*uncustomary*'. Bilal and I talked afterward about your use of the word '*uncustomary*' and I summoned Bilal with the following message, 'My brother, it is time to celebrate. I have found something *uncustomary*. I know it is late, but get here pm! Room 318.' He deciphered the 'uncustomary' and the 'pm' to refer to you, the Prime Minister. Without Bilal, Baker might have gotten away and I might have been his latest victim."

Bilal then asks, "What I don't understand is, how did you get Lizette here without Dublé knowing?"

I pause. No answer. I turn to Lizette, "Why did you come here?"

She smiles, "I was missing you."

Returning her smile, I ask, "So where'd you get the gun?"

"Sahar. She had it in her bag and wasn't allowed to take it on the plane. She handed it to me and said, '*Ukht*, let it serve you as it has served me.'"

Gazing into her beautiful browns eyes there are no doubts, "I love you Lizette."

"I love you too, Carter Dunstin."

THIRTY-THREE

Saturday, August 11, 2007, 8:17 P.M.

The coral reef around Djibouti in the Gulf d'Tadjoura is famous for its abundant underwater varieties. The beauty of the sun going down from the vantage point of the lounge chairs in front of the huts on Moucha Island majestically complement the wondrous display. Moucha Island is at our disposal for the weekend, compliments of President Mukhtar Sugal, who made us his special guest and personally honored us at Djibouti's 30th Independence Day celebration last month on the 27th. Ambassador Singleton and myself were awarded Djibouti's International Civilian Award, the highest honor given to Non-Djiboutians. Bilal, on the other hand, was awarded Djibouti's Expeditionary Medal for his work in helping to bring international attention to the resources of the country.

The weekend Presidential grant of Moucha Island is a nice story, but the reality is that we were given its exclusive use by

Prime Minister Diya al Din Hasani in exchange for our silence. It turned out that Djiboutian Royal Guard Waleed, the one who transcribed the conversation during the interrogation, was the link between Dublé and inside information concerning the whereabouts of the President, the Prime Minister and the Royal Guard Detail. Waleed also surrendered the schematic of the city's remote camera system, which included their frequency codes to Dublé. This information allowed Dublé to know the whereabouts of the cameras and to distort their images with a powerful but pocket-sized pre-set frequency jammer. For Waleed, the bride money was good but the passing grade given to his sister, a student at the Université, helped to maintain the crooked relationship.

It soon became evident that the mild mannered Professeur Henri Dublé, was living a double life. Intellectually helpful and stimulating by day but greedy, ruthless and conniving by night. He, and those in his network were responsible for over 9.5 million dollars in stolen diamonds being transported outside of the Kimberly Process. Diamonds from Sierra Leone, Liberia, the Ivory Coast, the Democratic Republic of Congo, and Angola were either mined illegally or stolen from legal mines with the owners executed. Many of these dirty diamonds were cut in Belgium. His international network of "businessman" cared little for human carnage and only for their material gain. The trade of these "conflict" or "blood diamonds" has resulted in the arming of rebel forces against recognized African governments and enabling thugs to prosper at the expense of fellow Africans. With pleasure and malice, he gained, while others suffered. The hard drive on his office and residence computers give details of the thefts, names, sellers, buyers, diamond routes, ledgers, and other forms of incriminating evidence that is linked to Dublé as Baker. The local verdict was quick. Guilty. He deserves death but will remain alive and tried on the international stage. Personally, I think they ought to let him rot in prison. His contempt is beyond understanding and his disregard for human life, beyond inhumane. Not only was he involved in the transport of dirty diamonds, but he was also responsible for other heinous crimes only to feed his selfishness.

Thus far, Dublé has shown no remorse. One bullet pierced his spine rendering him paralyzed from the waist down. The other bullet landed in his left buttocks. Yes, she shot him in the ass. He's been in the hospital and in prison for the last two months.

The main witnesses against Dublé were Henson "Ulysses" Perry, Boulos Adsir Aideed and the late Na'im. Henson is now free and is serving an inner-country house arrest arrangement in Djibouti City. The events that led to his being shot in the back, or upper shoulder, gives credibility to the notion that he was not a part of Dublés network of death and theft.

Boulos gave a detailed confession concerning his transgressions in league with his brother Butrus, and Dublé. The twin's involvement over the years in murders, rapes, maiming, and other human atrocities, placed them on an International Most Wanted List, deemed capable of "killing with no regard." My anger toward the silence in the community blinded me from the connection that these twin demons, were Law and Grace, they were the ones who senselessly ended the life of Maxi. They were the ones who held the entire Market Square in a consistent state of fear through intimidation. I wanted justice for Maxi and I was attempted to press charges separately but justice will not be served. Two weeks ago, Boulos was found in his cell, hanged by his bed sheet. Suicide it was ruled, heartbroken by the death of his twin brother. The issue of having his hands tied behind his back while hanging was another story all together.

The late Na'im also produced evidence that was used to convict Dublé. The computer that was found in his lair at Lac Assal, showed the routes of the tracking devices and despite their meandering throughout Africa and to a variety of other countries, they always lead to one of four places; the Market Square, the 112 Warehouse, Lac Assal and Dublés personal residence.

A search of the green van parked at the 112 Warehouse produced a rag with traces of chloroform. Test concluded that the chemical components of the $CHCl_3$ on the rag were a perfect match to that which was in the half-emptied container that was on the shelf in Dublés office.

Ironically, his own words provided the greatest testimony against him. The cassette recorder clearly captured every word of his boastful confession.

Sadly, the mindset for him and others was simply this, its Africa. The rules and laws that are internationally sufficient to maintain civility in America, Europe and other countries don't necessarily seem to apply in Africa. Through the ages, this mindset has worked to keep this great Continent in a functionally dysfunctional status. Raping the land and stealing the reserves have historically been the norm, but it cannot be ignored that the wrongs inflicted upon Africa are generally done with the help of other Africans. Thinking broadly, Dublé and the twins represented the relationship that other countries have had concerning the wealth from this great land.

Add to all of this, Dublés sorry butt actually tried to forward my research to the International Convention of Taxonomists and was claiming to have done the work. He bogusly forwarded pictures of my specimen, and tried to manufacture records. His efforts were ultimately thwarted because Dr. Heggie at Clarkmore was constantly updating his petition with the Convention, sure of the fact that we would achieve our goal of research importance.

As the sun nears it's descent on this glorious August day, the thoughts of everyone in the group are finding rest along with the setting of the life sustaining orb. Next to me is Lizette. My true soul mate. Our relationship has gone into overdrive and at this time when others would be moving head over heels to the next step, we remain committed, yet practical. She maintains her flat. I still live at the Menelik. She is still the best real estate agent in the region and she has won my heart in so many different ways. Most importantly, this girl can cook her sexy little booty off.

In the lounge chair next to Lizette is my mom. She came over to attend the Independence Day ceremonies and to help me to celebrate my find. She's also here making sure I don't mess up, concerning Lizette.

In the lounge chairs next to mom, is Ambassador Singleton and Lady Emmie. I never would have guessed that people in such high places could be so incredibly humble. When they visited the United States two months ago, the Ambassador made good on his promise. He personally informed President Bush, about me and my research in conjunction with Clarkmore University. During a Science and Technology Conference in Seattle, Washington the President then made mention of our efforts as an example of, "Americans who are constantly investigating the world, with the hope of making life better for all of mankind." Just the mention of my work, by the President, has resulted in nearly three million dollars in research funding exclusively for the Clarkmore University Research Department.

Next in the lounge chairs is Bilal and Numa. Normally, this wouldn't be, but Bilal's status in society has changed. Bilal has turned his new found fame into Open Excursions, their motto, "You need to get there. We'll take you." Numa is handling the office operation of their developing business and so far business is booming. We are collaborating on a paper about ways to utilize the resources at Lac Assal. The potential is huge and investors are eager. We are on the short list to present the same before the United Nations General Assembly in the near future.

As the top of the sun dances on the mountains on the horizon, I place my spiral notebook, containing two letters on the sand. One letter reads, "Thank you all for helping to give me a new start in life. My family is happy to have me home. I love each of you. Sahar." The other letter is from the International Convention of Taxonomist and it basically reads, "Congratulations on your discovery of *Hexagenius limbotus (Clarkmore)*, nicknamed, 'The Dunstin Fly.'"

Serenity abounds, then Numa asks, "Professeur Dunstin, explain to me why I had to spend my first night of marriage in the home of my parents without my husband?"

Bilal interrupts, "Numa, not here, not now." For a moment, a fleeting instant, it felt as if the sun delayed its descent, as an icy, sub-zero chill swept from out of the Gulf and over the Island as she responds to Bilal by giving him, "the look".

PLAYLIST

- **Aretha Franklin**, *Respect*, from "I Never Loved a Man the Way I Love You" (©1967).

- **Bootsy's Rubber Band**, *Bootzilla*, from "Bootsy? Player of the Year" (©1978).

- **Carl Orff**, *Fortuna Imperitrix Mundi ("O Fortuna")*, from "Carmina Barana" (©1936).

- **Charlie Daniels Band**, *The Devil went to Georgia*, from "Essential Super Hits" (©1979 and ©2004).

- **Dave Koz**, *Shakin' the Shack*, from "Lucky Man" (©1993)

- **Grover Washington,** *Mister Magic*, from "Mister Magic" ©1974).

- **James Baskett,** *Zip-a-Dee-Doo-Dah,* from **Disney's**, **"Song of the South"**, written by A. Wrobel, lyrics by R. Gilbert (©1946).

- **James Taylor**, *Something in the Way She Moves*, from "James Taylor" (© 1968).

- **Jimi Hendrix**, *Born Under A Bad Sign*, from "Blues" (©1994).

- **Kirk Franklin**, *Stomp*, from "God's Property" (©1997).

- **Lionel Richie**, *Three Times A Lady*, from "Back to Front" (©1992).

- **Michael Jackson**, *Man in the Mirror*, from "Bad" (©1987).

- **Old Negro Spiritual**, Anon, (Public Domain).

- **Bobby McFerrin,** *Don't Worry, Be Happy* from "Simple Pleasures" (© 1988).

<u>GLOSSARY</u>

<u>Arabic Translations</u>

Subax wanaagsan - good morning

Al Masjid - Mosque

madrasa 'amal - school work

shukran - Thank you

afwan - Don't mention it.

As-salaamu alaikum - Peace is upon you.

Wa 'alaikum as-salaam - Upon you be peace.

Wa 'alaikum as-salaam wa-raHumat ulaahi wa barakaatuh - And peace is upon you too, as well as God's mercy and his blessings.

macawiis – traditional sarong-like manskirt

al-qaanoon - Law

rashaaqa - Grace

Akh - brother

Ukht - sister

qahwa - coffee

A'taqid an al-iSaaba jaseema - I think the injury is serious.

yaqif - stand or stop

Gaacmaha kor utaag - hands up

Hubka dhig - lay down your weapons

joogso - don't move, halt

WaaDiH - obvious or clear

iHtiraam - respect

Yatakal-lam - talk or speak

Magacaa - What is your name?

Maxaad radtaa - What do you want?

Iaq raali ahaw - Excuse me

maas - diamonds

Idaara - Administration

Qadâ - makeup for missed prayer

uTlubu l-is'aaf - Call an ambulance!

Yuraaqib - Watch!

Salah (or Salat) – the name of the formal prayer of Islam. The centrality of prayer in the life of Muslims cannot be understated, Salah is one of the Five Pillars of Sunni Islam and one of the Ten Practices of the Religion of Shi'a Islam. Salah is ritual prayer and it is performed at prescribed times, it has prescribed conditions, and it follows prescribed procedures.

Tradition holds that Salah be performed five times a day. The actual time of prayer is measured by the movement of the sun. Traditionally, the muezzin announces the call to prayer from the minaret of the mosque, but today the call can also be heard on the radio. Salah is performed at near dawn (fajr), just after the sun's noon, or midday (zuhr or dhuhr), in the afternoon (asr), just after sunset (maghrib) and around nightfall (isha'a).

Prayers are always directed toward the Ka'ba Shrine in Mecca. Ritual washing, called ablutions, of the hands, feet and face precede prayer. The actual prayers contain verses from the Qur'an and are said in Arabic, "the language of the Revelation."

Here are the words of the **shahada** which are prominent in the call to prayer:

Allahu Akbar (God is most great)
Ashadu anna la ilaha illa Allah (I bear witness there is no god but God)
Ashadu anna Muhammadan rasul Allah (I bear witness Muhammad is the prophet of God)
Haiya 'ala al-Salah (Come to prayer)
Haiya 'ala ai-falah (Come to wellbeing)
Al-Salah khayrun min al-nawn (Prayer is better than sleep)
Allahu Akbar (God s most great)
La ilaha illa Allah (There is no God but God)

The preferred place to worship is in a mosque, but Muslims may pray anywhere, in fields, offices, deserts, anywhere. Salah is structured, but personal prayers can be offered at any time.

<u>WARNING!</u>

KHAT IS AN ILLEGAL SUBSTANCE IN THE UNITED STATES AND SHOULD NOT BE TESTED OR SAMPLED UNDER ANY CIRCUMSTANCES. Destructive physical changes can easily result from khat use. Some harmful effects include irregular cardio-vascular rhythms, impeded sexual function, digestive disorders, and of course, dental complications.